THE MADDY SAGA

BOOK TEN

PONYGIRL'S FATE

BY

PAUL BLADES

Cover Art by Amy Row
amyrow.com

Dark Visions Publications
darkvisionspub@gmail.com

Other Books by Paul Blades:

CHAPTER ONE

Chocolate moaned with pleasure as the warm lips of the blond haired, Latvian slave girl, Ilona, ran her able tongue along the course of her dilated, engorged labia and sucked on her stiffened clit. She caressed the insides of her thighs with her delicate, gentle hands as she dragged her tongue slowly and sensually deeply along the divide between the ponygirl's plush love lips. The slave girl's tongue had a deft touch, and when she flicked it against the pony's stiffened love bud, it created an agonizingly pleasurable sensation that made the tall, strong, former woman moan and her knees sag. When Chocolate's thighs began to shake and her hips began to thrust urgently at the mouth that tormented her, Ilona withdrew, stood, and, after giving the pony affectionate kisses on her long, fat, hardened nipples, went back to her work.

Fifteen minutes or so later, the slave girl was be back on her knees worshiping at the pony's slit, bringing her to the brink of completion, but no further. The ponygirl groaned with frustration each time the slave girl abandoned her task. But Chocolate knew that she would not receive completion of her lusts this morning. There was work to be done.

To say that the tall, strong, brown skinned ponygirl was overwhelmed by the experience of being at the Fall Pony-girl Tournament would have been a vast understatement. Of course, everything about having become a ponygirl was overwhelming, her permanently hooded face, the denial of the use of her arms, her eternal enforced silence. But this was of a different degree and of a different nature. Tethered to the seven foot high, thick, round pole that stood in the middle of the campsite, she watched as dozens of naked and hooded ponies kept passing their little temporary homestead, pulling carts or on leads held by pretty, naked, little slave girls. Chocolate marveled at the number of ponies that she saw. No one had told her, no one told ponygirls anything, but she had concluded that they were at the Fall Tournament campground and that the drama for which she had been recruited was, at long last, about to begin.

The ride to the Fall Tournament grounds had been a long, boring one. Her trailer, in which she had been bound standing and facing the front wall, was hot and dusty. Although the back of her trailer was wide open, the chain that connected her gag tautly to the trailer wall in front of her prevented her from turning to enjoy the view. It would have been more tolerable if she could have watched the countryside go by, but those kinds of considerations were not made for ponygirls.

Because of the variation in her routines, the shapely, big breasted pony had been sure something special was happening even before she had started on her journey. She had had two full days of rest from her exertions, the first time she had not raced or trained for two days in a row since she had been transformed from a woman into a beast. There was an excitement around the camp that was palpable. Her driver's slave girl had been especially indulgent and warm to her. Her pussy had been well attended to and she was allowed to suck at her driver's cock a couple of times a day.

It was dark when they arrived at the tournament ponypark. She was immediately pulled from her trailer and laid to rest under it, her body cocooned by a heavy blanket for the cold night, her thighs and ankles bound, chains leading from her collar and ankles to rings pounded into the ground on either side of her. She had gotten used to sleeping this way, her arms laying flat underneath her back, her hood's eyelets closed. It accentuated the total control that her masters had over her and she had long since learned to accept it.

The morning brought a whole world of new sights. During the racing season, estate teams would be matched against each other, for the most part, one on one, although from time to time the smaller estates who fielded only one or two teams were allowed to participate. She would see the other team's ponies before the race, but they all uniformly wore the same color hood and their carts were all bedecked with the identical pennant proudly displaying the emblem of the estate to which they belonged. The ponies that she saw from her perch now were wearing a wide variety of colored hoods, red, orange, blue, and many multicolored ones. The faceless, former women were all in tip top form and eminently graceful. This was, after all, the cream of the crop, the winners of many previous races, the best ponygirls in the world. Chocolate saw at least a dozen different pennants as the ponies were driven by on their way to their morning exercise. Although she had always felt that the ponygirl world she was immersed in was surreal, she had not perceived its scale until now.

She had been awoken early and cleaned and fed by her pretty, slave girl attendant. After she was rehooded and ready for the day, she was tethered to the large pole where she stood. That is how Chocolate spent the hour or so while waiting for her own upcoming exercise session. She didn't know that that was what she was waiting for of course; she just knew that, as much of her time was spent, she was waiting for something or someone. You couldn't let ponies just wander around or lie or kneel down for extended periods on training or racing days. It made them sluggish and lazy. Mounted, as Chocolate was now, also made a pony available for easy discipline with a quirt or a rod, or for sexual servicing, a slave girl kneeling between its extended thighs, lapping at its gate of pleasure.

Giorgi, her dwarfish driver, had left Ilona strict instruct-tions. There would be no orgasms for Chocolate until the last race had been run and then only if she won the ultimate victory, a championship. She would face a severe session with the whip if she did not. As an added incentive to the former woman to excel, and to create a finely honed edge to her temperament, she would be kept in a continual state of high sexual tension.

So, several times in the hour and a half that Chocolate stood with her collar connected to the pole by a short chain, a spreader bar keeping her ankles two feet apart, Ilona knelt between her powerful, bronze thighs and worshiped at her plump, hairless mons.

When Chocolate was not moaning with anguished frustration at the interruption of her path to climax, she reminisced about the strange path that had led her to this moment. It had been a hard, painful road for the former Chicago hooker. Jake, the tough, resourceful and generally honorable fixer who worked for her owner, the American billionaire, Michael Burnham, had proffered to her the opportunity to make a million dollars if she consented to become a ponygirl. It was part of a plan to rescue Burnham's kidnapped niece, Maddy, who had been transported to Kalikastan and turned into a ponygirl. Jake had warned her that she would have to endure five months of hard work and cruel treatment, and that she couldn't understand what it meant to be a ponygirl until she had been to Kalikastan. "Fuckin' eh, right!" she thought now as she mulled over her experiences since being dehumanized. She didn't know how the other ponies, who faced a lifetime of dreadful embondment, handled it. Her own debasement and dehumanization was attenuated by the belief that after she had done her best to defeat Maddy in a match race, she would be going home, win or lose. Jake had promised it and Jake always kept his promises.

Nonetheless, it had been hard to have been deprived of human status for so long. Every day, she led her bound hands through deliberate exercises, flexing and clasping her fingers into fists to maintain her consciousness of them and their future usefulness. Every time that she was beaten or whipped, and it was often, she ameliorated her pain and humiliation by the thought of the house she wanted to buy on the Pacific coast where she could wile away her days doing nothing except whatever she wanted to and where no one would ever have control over her ever again.

She did have to admit that her days were filled with exhilaration. Her body had never felt so strong or well toned, even as a high school track star. The sex was outstanding, it being thought that a diet of regular orgasms, sometimes up to ten a day, made the ponies compliant and inured to their new status. To a large extent it was true. That was what made being deprived of her usual regimen of ecstatic pleasure now so hard. Her mind and body yearned for it almost hourly.

The thrill of running a race, even as a faceless animal, her hands bound behind her, naked for all the world to see, was intense. Chocolate reveled in victory, and she had proven a hard, determined competitor who hated to see the back of another pony during a race.

She had, initially, been trained to run the 1500 meter sulky, thought by many to be the pinnacle of ponygirl racing. The strategy was that she would be matched against Maddy, now known as Lightning, at the end of the season in the Fall Championship. But Lightning had been switched unexpectedly to the 3000 meter race. So the strategy changed and it was decided by Jake and Burnham that they would challenge Lightning's owner, Axmail Grobgy, a powerful Russian gangster, to a claiming race after the tournament. That meant that Chocolate would have to train for the longer race as well. And it required that both ponies champion in their respective classes.

Training for two races at the same time had been hard. Chocolate had not been told that that was what she was doing. She had finally figured it out after being brought over surreptitiously to the training track at the Burnham estate every day that they were there to learn to run full speed for two circuits around the 1500 meter oval. It would have been a lot easier if they had told her that she was training to best Maddy in a 3000 meter match race, but that was not the Kalikastani way. No one ever spoke to her, except for the one or two word Russian commands she learned the meaning of after some harsh lessons with the whip, or the mysterious, but soothing, foreign words sometimes whispered to her by the pretty, young, slave girl who attended her. Chocolate had been raised on the streets of Chicago, though, and knew what a ringer was. She was a ringer, no doubt, and she knew she would give the white skinned pony a run for her money when they finally met.

It was when she was driven down to the tournament track for her morning exercise that Chocolate had her real moment of awe. As they passed through the ponypark, Chocolate's sense of amazement grew with every step. There were dozens and dozens of encampments, all filled with hooded, naked ponygirls. The thoroughfares of the encampment were divided into two lanes to accommodate the traffic.

There was a little hill that you had to traverse between the campgrounds and the grandstands. When she pulled her cart over the top of it she got a glimpse through the dime sized holes of her black, Neoprene hood of the vast expanse of the festival campgrounds and the thousands of people there. It took her breath away. She quickly descended the hill towards the huge grandstand. Large flags waved from the top of it, each one denoting an estate that had ponies at the meet. In the middle, and standing the tallest, was the black and red Kalikastan flag with its mailed fist in the center. Near the end, on the right, was the flag of her estate, the head of a vicious, snarling, black mastiff on a field of red. It was the same mastiff that she wore tattooed on her lower belly.

Every type of carriage that was used in ponygirl racing seemed to be on the track at once. Hundreds of people were lined up at the rails to watch the naked ponygirls go through their drills. There was an air of high tension and excitement that Chocolate found thrilling.

Each pony team had its own prescribed practice time. Coordination of the many teams was very important. It wouldn't do for all the 9 pony landaus, for instance, to be running on the track at once. There were ten teams in each division at the tournament. Ten large landaus with their three by three, large, powerful ponygirls hauling them on the track at the same time would have been a recipe for disaster.

Chocolate's driver guided her out onto the well groomed, smooth, dirt track and signaled her into a quick trot. To her amazement, she heard her name called out by several of the onlookers as she passed them. Not her former human name, Jackie, of course, but her new name, in Russian, *Shokoladniy*. She had heard the masters call her that and had heard her name shouted out after several of her victiories during the racing season. It was etched in two inch high, Cryllic letters on her chest above her breasts. She had deduced its meaning from its phonetic similarity to the word in English and, of course, the color of her skin.

In fact, *Shokoladniy* was the buzz of the tournament, along with her fellow American pony, *Molnya*, or Lightning. Everyone who knew anything knew about the prospective showdown between the two new, fast ponies. Some players were already making book on the race even though it had not been announced formally or even specifically agreed to by the parties. *Molnya* was given 7 to 5 odds currently to beat the brown skinned *Shokoladniy*. This was down from 8 to 5 because of the rumours about an injury to *Molnya*'s foot. The smart money still felt, however, that the pale skinned pony's greater experience in the 3000 meter race would be the deciding factor. Others, having heard about or seen *Shokoladny's* heroic race against *Ninotchka* on a mud strewn track two weeks earlier, were putting their money on the brown skinned yearling.

Chocolate was so dazed by the number and variety of carriages being hauled around the track and the festive atmosphere of the crowd, that she failed to note her driver's instructions through the reins that led to the leather covered, steel bit in her mouth to increase her pace. A fierce crack of the whip on her back brought her around and she immediately quickened.

It was not unusual for the ponies to be a little off their game when they first entered the tournament track. It was the reason that their pre-race workouts were so important, so that when they came out on race day their jitters were behind them and they could concentrate on their task at hand. It didn't always work and many times a crowd favorite had gone down to defeat because the pony or ponies were disconcerted by the huge crowds and the concomitant excitement. It was one of the reasons that the events were double elimination. This way a pony or team of ponies would still have a chance to overcome their jitters and run the races they were truly capable of.

Giorgi brought the pony three times around the track at half speed. Her brown skin was shiny with sweat from her exertions and her long, brown ponytail flipped back and forth as she ran. On the fourth lap, he brought her up to ¾ speed, mostly for the benefit of the cheering audience. After giving her a cool off run, he brought her back to the ponypark. There would be another practice run in the late afternoon.

When they returned to their encampment, Giorgi had the pony tied back up to her post without waiting for her harness to be removed or for her to receive the customary rubdown from Ilona. He had noticed the sluggishness of the pony, her hesitation in obeying commands. He knew that its attention needed to be brought back to the task at hand and that it needed a refresher on the consequences of failure.

Chocolate saw her driver retrieve the long, thin quirt from its hook next to the door to his camper. Her stomach quailed as she watched him approach her, swinging it back and forth in the air. Like most of the ponies, Chocolate had never gotten used to the fact of being subject to the whip. Her back still smarted from where she had been whipped out on the track. But that had been a mere glancing blow compared to what the dwarfish driver was now going to administer. She knew that she deserved it, had, in fact, earned it by her distracted performance, but that didn't make her one iota more prepared to accept it.

Giorgi, like his brother, Jerzi, being only a mite over four feet tall, used a stool when he wanted to slash a whip across the breasts of his charge. Ilona bought it out now. She placed it about four feet in front of the whining, distraught pony. Giorgi hopped up onto it and without ceremony, laid the whip harshly across the pony's large, firm, round breasts.

Chocolate's whole body cringed when the pain from the meeting of the cruel leather with the tender skin of her mammaries shot through her. A fire lit up across them. "Oooooooooooouu!" she called out. Her knees sagged and the short chain that held her ponygirl collar affixed to the post behind her tautened. Her driver laid it on again and again. Five times the lash bit into her flesh, sending agonizing sensations of pain through her body. Giorgi was an expert with the lash and he made sure that each searing blow had the maximum effect. Bright red lines emerged on the pony's flesh, across her breasts, her belly and her thighs. The whip made a sickening slapping sound as it made contact, followed quickly by a piteous moan from the tall, ebony creature.

Behind the black hood that hid her face, tears streamed down Chocolate's cheeks. Her lips could be seen attempting a frown, inhibited by the cruelly devised bit that kept them spread into a grotesque grimace. Her wounds burned. A feeling of deep humiliation and self pity filled her. No animal was treated as cruelly as a ponygirl.

The pony continued to shiver in fear and pain even as Giorgi flung the whip aside and descended from his small perch. He dragged the stool closer to his victim and, standing on it once again, reached up and lowered the Velcro flaps to her black hood, sealing her into darkness. Chocolate would be able to meditate upon her brief, sharp lesson without distractions.

The diminutive ponygirl driver hopped off the stool and signaled to his slave girl to put it away. He went over to his caravan and sat in his favorite chair. Ilona had, as per her standing instructions, put out a bottle of vodka for him and a small glass. He poured himself a shot and took it down quickly.

Whipping the pony always got his passions up and this time was no different. His man sized cock was hard and yearning for attention. When his big breasted, blond slave girl was done putting away the stool he motioned for her to approach him. He fished out his stiffened wand from his pants. The pretty, naked girl needed no instructions about what to do. She knelt between his short but muscular thighs and took his fat prick between her lips.

Giorgi moaned as the warm, wet, enslaved mouth brought him pleasure. Ilona was an expert cocksucker. Her tongue tantalized his pole as her tight lips rode up and down it. Her strokes were long and languorous, beginning with a suckle at the bulbous head and then descending until the fleshy helmet breached her throat and her face mashed up against her master's taut belly.

While his body was enjoying the efforts of his slave, his eyes were washing over the form of his tall, brown skinned pony. Her body was beautiful, with plump, round breasts that were still swaying and shivering as the pony recovered from its ordeal. Her spread thighs revealed the smooth, hairless, tawny mound in which he had, over the last eight weeks, found much enjoyment. He would deny himself the pleasure of the pony's body for the next three days. If she lost, he would not fuck her again. That thought made him anxious and more determined than ever to bring her to victory. He laid his hand on the blond head that was pleasuring him. The slave girl would have to do for now. Soon, she would be replaced. One of those pretty, young, black slave girls the Americans were importing maybe next, he thought. Their shiny, black skin seemed so alluring and exotic to him. Pietrov, a fellow driver, had one and Giorgi was jealous of him.

As the female's efforts began to suffuse his body with a pleasurable glow, he realized how tense he had been. It was lucky he had the mouth of a pretty slave girl to take the edge off. Like most ponygirl drivers, Giorgi was a master of sexual control. If he didn't want to come, the poor slave girl could suck at his wand all day long with no result. Right now, he needed the release. He allowed the exquisite sensations of the well trained lips and tongue carry him over the threshold of pleasure. When he came, he groaned long and hard as Ilona consumed very drop of his thick, white sauce.

That afternoon, about 4 p.m., just as the sun started slipping down behind the looming Carpathian Mountains to the west, Chocolate was brought out for her afternoon run. The whipping had done the trick. She responded to the reins like a well tuned Ferrari. They were ready.

* * * * * * * * * * * * *

The tension in the air was palpable when Chocolate was awoken the next morning. Giorgi was, uncharacteristically, up early too. Chocolate had heard him and the slave girl going at it in the trailer above her during the night like teenagers. The sound of them fucking accentuated her tense, frustrated state. She had been brought to the edge of orgasm repeatedly during the day and after dinner. Lying under the trailer, awaiting sleep, she had rubbed her thighs together tightly, trying to squeeze her pussy to pleasure between them. Now, after her shower and the ritualistic shaving of her head and loins, Ilona had her on her back with her knees spread wing like on either side of her and was teasing her stiffened clit with her tongue. Chocolate's thighs shuddered with need. When her belly began to rise and fall excitedly, her breath becoming long and labored, the slave girl rose to her knees and patted her trilling loins.

Chocolate realized how much her heightened desire for sexual completion drove her success as a ponygirl. It gave her an intense feeling of need that let her concentrate all of her effort on the only thing that would bring her relief, victory. It was hard, but necessary. She realized that. But it did not make the powerful feelings of frustration any easier to bear.

Ilona brought the pony to her feet and began to adorn her with her racing regalia. The sulky had been painted and polished to showroom standards. Bright black and gold ribbons festooned the wheels and the contours of the cart. A gold pennant with the black, ferocious head of a mastiff adorning it had been mounted behind the driver's seat. It was a little before seven o'clock. The ponies would start lining up for the opening parade scheduled for 8, very soon.

Giorgi had donned his racing outfit, the quartered, black and gold cap, blouse and pants. His black boots were shined to a glossy glow. He watched Ilona strap the racing harness on his pony nervously. He hated the pomp and ceremony of the pony parade on the first day of the tournament. It was a long and drawn out affair. There were seven divisions to race, the nine pony landau, the six pony cabriolet, the four pony brougham, the three pony troika, the two pony yearling cart and the 1500 and 3000 meter sulkies. At ten teams to a division, that meant a parade of 70 pony teams in the parade, 250 ponies in all.

It took a half hour for the teams to cross in front of the grandstand where the owners and the racing officials sat in their luxury boxes and enjoyed the display of indentured, naked, former women strutting obediently before them. It was a great crowd pleaser too, and the fans would start very early filling either the reserved boxes, the general admission seats or the standing room in the broad open area next to the rail. The track was licensed for 7500 people, although the fire codes were not strictly enforced. Last spring it was all assholes and elbows as the tournament set a new record on the day of the finals with paid attendance at a little over 8,700 fans.

The early start of the parade enabled the races to get off early as well. With a double elimination program, it could take a long time to get them all in. Depending on the outcome of the individual heats, there could be as many as four heats in a day for a single team. Most teams would win at least one victory, although the seeding system did work to weed out the less accomplished teams quickly.

The second day of the tournament separated the wheat from the chaff. It was run from 8 a.m. to whenever there were only two teams left in each division. Sometimes tiebreakers had to be run as well. On the third day, there would be just the finals.

When Ilona had Chocolate mounted properly in front of the cart, Giorgi locked the naked slave girl's bracelets behind her back and had her kneel down on the ground. He clipped the bracelets on her ankles together and adorned her with her gag. Unless someone spirited her away, she would be right where he left her when he got back.

He stepped up to the tall, broad shouldered, deep tan skinned pony. His head came up to just the level of her fat, round nipples. He placed his hand between her thighs, rubbing the soft flesh there until he felt her moisture begin to flow. When the pony issued a deep sigh and her hips began to sway, her removed his hand and gave her an affectionate swat on her rear haunches. "Okay, *Shokoladniy*," he said to her in Russian, "let's go."

* * * * * * * * * * * * * *

Not far away, another pony was being eased back into her traces in preparation for the parade. Lightning's foot was still a problem. Her driver's former attendant, Natasha, resentful at being enslaved and forced to service the dehumanized, former woman, had cruelly and surreptitiously placed a stone in Lightning's boot, something she did regularly to harass her and cause her discomfort. Unfortunately, this time the stone tore a hole in the sole of Lightning's foot, practically disabling her. Natasha paid for her foolishness with her life. Lightning's foot, while not fully healed, had been specially wrapped and given time to rest. She had not run any of her exercise sessions and had, uncharacteristically, been allowed to stay off her feet during the long drive to the ponygirl grounds. Luckily, her first two races would be against weak runners in low seeds. She would not have to go all out until perhaps her third race of the day.

Lightning's new slave girl attendant was named Amanda. A former, spoiled, British, rich girl, Amanda's skill at taking care of her had grown exponentially since Jerzi had had her whip Lightning the night before. It was the first time the full breasted, black haired slave girl had ever whipped anyone, never mind a ponygirl. It had been exhilarating and, she realized, now made her complicit in the ponygirl's subjugation. While Amanda was still kind and tender with the pony's flesh, using tantalizingly soft and gentle strokes to rub in the daily ointment on her pale, sun deprived face, or solicitous while shaving the sensitive skin of her pudenda and scalp, she had acquired the taste of command. Instead of urging the pony to its feet with soft, comforting, almost apologetic words, she now clapped her hands twice and shouted out in Russian, "Oop!! Oop!"

The feeling that she was again being handled by someone of competence and inner strength was comforting to Lightning.

Jerzi was still in his trailer putting on his racing outfit. Lightning was mounted in her harness and affixed to the cart. She wore a blue and gold hood and a blue feathered plume on her head. Amanda had painted her nipples a dark maroon and had outlined the lines of her labia as well. It was light enough so that at a distance you would not be sure whether it was the pony's natural colorings or not, but dark enough so that her feminine qualities would be quite brazenly accentuated. Natasha, Jerzi's prior slave girl, the one who had put the stone in her shoe which caused her injury, had never adorned Lightning like that. Although she couldn't see the shading of her intimate parts, Lightning knew that they had been especially decorated and she imagined the starkness with which her nakedness would be displayed to the crowd. When Jerzi had seen it earlier, he laughed aloud and patted the slave girl on the head. God knows where she got the lipstick from, he thought. Slave girls were a mystery after all.

While they waited for Jerzi to emerge, Amanda had her palm pressed against the puffy flesh of Lightning's pudenda and her fingers were delicately taunting the flesh of its divide. She looked up at the 5' 10" tall pony leeringly. Fulfilling her duty to bring pleasure to the ponygirl had taught her for the first time what men felt when they handled her body. She had no right to refuse them as the pony had no right to refuse her. She had often wondered why they went to so much trouble to kidnap and enslave young women when there were so many of them out there ready to put out for free or for the price of a good meal. She had her answer right there. Her own passion rose as she detected the nascent signs of arousal in the pony under her power. Its cleft was moist and soft and its hips trembled slightly. Its breath had become short and ragged. Like Chocolate, Lightning would not enjoy the satisfaction of an orgasm until and unless she came back a champion.

The saucy girl relished the thought of taunting and teasing the pony's flesh for the next three days as she had been instructed by her master. As long as she got to play with the little man's magic prick when she was done that is. All of her life, Amanda had been looking for her place, somewhere that she felt at home. Now in the midst of her new depravity, she had finally found it.

Lightning squirmed and moaned as the young girl's fingers enflamed her. Her foot was still sore where it had been injured and she hoped that it would not hold her back. She had won the 1500 meter championship at the

Spring Tournament and she wanted desperately to win another gold medal, to be the best. Why else endure all that she endured? What else could otherwise possibly justify her obeisance and compliance with all of the outrageous acts committed upon her? At the moment, that was far from her mind though as her desire and need for sexual fulfillment was growing higher and higher. "Make it last a little longer! Don't stop, please don't stop!" she thought frantically.

When Jerzi emerged from his trailer, Amanda withdrew her hand. She took one of Lightning's large breasts in her hand and gave it a gentle kiss to show that it had all been in good fun. At Jerzi's command, she turned and put her hands behind her. Once her braceleted wrists had been clipped together, she knelt and let him fasten her ankles to each other and then gag her. She too would be just where she was left when her master retuned.

The small but powerful man approached his pony. He rubbed his large, scarred, strong hands along the fronts of her thighs and gave her moist love lips a single caress. With a gesture, he commanded the pony to kneel. It was difficult, but not impossible to do while hitched to the cart and Lightning obeyed immediately. He took something out of his pocket and dangled it in front of her eyes. It was her gold championship medal from the Spring Tournament, which he had taken away from her at the beginning of the fall racing season. He fastened it to her collar. Lightning would march in the ponygirl parade as the champion that she was. She deserved no less.

She had earned the medal, proved herself a class above all the rest, at least at one time, in one season. In three days, they would know whether it was more than a flash of brilliance. For it took more than speed and physical strength to become a ponygirl champion. It took strength of will, a hatred of defeat, a need for exaltation. This pony had it all right. He clipped the medal to the pony's collar and ordered her to rise. He walked behind her, swung himself up on the cart and, with a flick of the reins, started her forward.

* * * * * * * * * * * * *

Across the fair grounds, in a large, luxurious tent in the restricted camp area, a tall, lithe, young woman with long black hair and pale white skin was confronting a naked slave girl. The girl was standing on her tip toes, with the bracelets around her wrists tied off to a tent pole above her. She was gagged and the woman before her, her mistress, had a whip in her hand.

Anya was pissed. Her lover, Anton Drabik, had deserted her again. She had sent word to urge him to come and fuck her in her tent last night, but he had told her messenger that it was, "too dangerous." Well fuck him and fuck her father who kept her so cock-deprived, she thought. And fuck this little fuck-up of a slave girl who spoiled all of her plans.

The callous, depraved, young woman was the daughter of the gangster Axmail Grobgy. While she was free to use and abuse any of her father's many slave girls, he drew the line at coitus with a male partner. He was wary lest some up and coming gangster took it into his head that he was the heir to his criminal empire. Such an expectation could lead very quickly to a belief that the younger gangster's reign should start sooner rather than later. He would have to shoot his own son-in-law.

Anya had been, nonetheless, carrying on a torrid affair with Drabik, her father's current right hand man and a proficient killer and ponygirl trainer. It was Drabik who had first trained and named Lightning. In the process, he had developed an obsession for the pony's flesh and she for his, something that did not sit well with Anya at all. One did not fall in love with a ponygirl who was, after all, a mere animal. Anya had tried several strategies to drive the two unlikely lovers apart to no avail. Now, she was having trouble getting Drabik into her bed at all.

Natalie, the slender, petit, former Hungarian shop girl who had been Anya's personal body slave for the last six months or so had failed her. She had strung her up in a fit of pique this morning after having to spend the night, again, alone in her bed. The slave girl looked at her piteously, knowing full well from personal experience Anya's skill with a whip. She was blubbering her imprecations for mercy through her gagged mouth. Anya, ignoring her muffled pleas, took the whip, a many tailed assembly of leather straps capped with sharp steel ends, and cruelly slashed it across the slave girl's exposed and defenseless breasts. She screamed in pain and her body stiffened. A multiple trail of red lines appeared across the small, tender orbs. Anya gave her another blow with her backhand, slicing through the flesh on her taut belly, across the fierce tattoo of a wolverine placed there. The girl screamed again, her agony spilling out of her confined mouth and resounding throughout the tent and outside. No one would pay it any mind. They would just figure a slave was being disciplined and shrug their shoulders. But it was more than that. Anya was red hot.

"I told you to get close to that stupid slave girl that took care of Lightning, didn't I?" Anya snarled at the helpless girl. "You said you would do it, knew where you could meet with her to convince her to help us. But did you do it? Noooooo, you didn't! You fucked up!"

Anya circled behind the distraught girl and slashed at the pristine skin of her back. The girl's sobs had become hysterical as she absorbed the pain. Thrice more, Anya let the cruel implement dash against the girl's flesh, across her rear, the back of her thighs and on her rump again. Blood trickled down where the spikes had dragged across her skin powered by the strong arm of the cruel, young woman.

"And last night, my lover, the one you were supposed to entice, did not come to my bed! Do you think that I have to put up with such an incompetent, stupid slave girl? Do you!" Anya scoured the girl's body again with the two foot long whip, causing her to howl from behind her gag and leaving deep, angry red lines across her breasts.

The girl was charged with forming a conspiracy with Natasha, Jerzi's former slave girl, to sabotage Lightning's rigging just before her upcoming match race against Chocolate. That would have insured her loss and her being shipped off to another estate where she could no longer bedevil the passions and lusts of Anya's lover. The plan had gone awry when the girl was caught putting stones in the pony's boot before Anya's slave girl could talk to her.

It had been impossible for the small, brown haired girl, Natalie, to get into the pony camp to speak with her. She had tried three times only to be caught and whipped for being out of bounds. "I tried mistress! I really tried! Please don't whip me! Please!" her mind screamed as the rapacious woman abused her. "Plllleeeeease!" she tried to scream through her gag.

Anya's passions were afire as they always got when she administered a whip to subservient female flesh. Her father,

Axmail, gave her free reign with the slave girls. It was cock that he drew the line at. But it was cock that Anya wanted most. Not any cock. Anton Drabik's! Now she would have to figure another way to get at the pony, right here in the middle of the tournament where security was so strict. Sure, as the daughter of an estate owner and master of three teams at the tournament, she could gain admission to the pony park. But her presence would certainly be noticed. If anything happened to the pony afterwards, she would be at the top of Drabik's list of suspects. She needed a plan. It was clear that this stupid slut was not up to the task.

Anya tossed the whip aside and freed the girl's hands from the pole above her. Natalie collapsed to the floor in a heap. "Get up!" Anya yelled as she kicked her with her shiny, black boot. "Get on your knees!" Anya was dressed in a long, woolen, black skirt and a crisp, white blouse. Black and white were her colors, matching her raven colored hair and her pale skin. Her eyes were dark brown, almost black, and woe betides a slave girl when fire flew out of them.

Natalie crept slowly to her knees. Anya, who had fire in her loins now too, unbuckled her skirt and stepped out of it. She rarely wore anything so confining as panties. Her sex had a fine, black trim of hair around it. Her legs were long, lean and well shaped. "Get over here and suck my pussy!" she ordered the girl.

Thankful that her ordeal was over and hoping that she could get back into her mistress's good graces, Natalie crawled towards her. Anya had spread her thighs apart in anticipation of the slave girl's services. Kneeling between her legs, her head tilted back, her hands still bound in front of her, Natalie began her oral adoration of Anya's crevasse. She ran her tongue upwards from her perineum to her clit and then back again. She buried her tongue inside the plush puss and mouthed the young woman's outer lips. She soon had her mistress in a paroxysm of passion. Anya grabbed the back of Natalie's head and pressed her firmly into her cunt. "Suck it hard, slut!" she yelled.

"You're the slut," Natalie thought as she obeyed her mistress's command. "You're the one who can't get enough. I'm just a slave girl."

Anya's breath came hard and fast. Her hips rocked against the mouth that serviced her. She could feel the tightness of her breasts and the fire in her belly. When the slave girl took her nubbin between her lips and began to suck on it, Anya moaned deeply with delight. She shouted out as she came, ignoring the possibility that people outside her tent might hear her. Her hips rocked and her knees buckled. She had hold of Natalie's head with both hands and she sought to bury the face between her thighs deep within her portal of pleasure.

Anya sighed deeply as she recovered her senses. The tongue of the subservient, young woman continued to lap at her essences. But Anya had had enough. She shoved the head back from her loins.

"What am I going to do with you?" she asked Natalie harshly. "You're an incompetent slut and you know too much. I know how you slave girls talk to each other. It's a regular telephone line. I'm going to have to shut you up." If Drabik ever found out that she had been trying to harm the ponygirl, he might kill her.

Anya leaned over and picked up the discarded gag from the floor of the sumptuous tent. The rug was a dark red oriental, with black trimmings. A silk covered, double bed lay centered against one wall and other fine furnishings lay strewn about. One was a finely woven wicker basket about three by three feet large. Anya had an idea.

She went over to the basket, which contained a supply of her clothes and dumped it over, emptying it. "Get in!" she told the child-like slave. "Get in or I'll whip you again."

"Please don't mistress, Natalie cried out. "I'll do it, mistress, I'll do it!"

She crawled across the tent and, rising from her knees, climbed into the basket. She just fit.

"Give me your mouth," Anya ordered curtly.

Natalie knelt up from her crouch and opened her mouth dutifully. Anya slid the long, thick leather prong home and then buckled the belt around the girl's head. The leather shield over the prong covered her face from her nostrils to the underside of her chin.

"Now get down!" Anya commanded.

Frightened as to her mistress's purpose, but more frightened of the whip, Natalie bent over until her whole body lay inside the trunk. Anya closed the lid and locked it.

After redonning her skirt, Anya stepped outside of the tent. Two of her father's security men were standing nearby. "Come here!" she snarled. Anya had no use for any of her father's servants. She respected only power and these men had none. She invited them inside the tent.

"You see that basket?" she asked the guards. They both nodded. "I want you to bury it six feet deep somewhere outside the fairgrounds. Anyplace that you can find. Got it?"

The men looked at each other. A squawking had commenced from inside the basket. Natalie did not want to go quietly into the night.

"Okay," one of them said. She was the boss's daughter and who cared what happened to a slave girl anyway? The two men picked up the basket by its side handles and carried it out. Frantic moans emanated from it. Anya smoothed her skirt and looked at her makeup in a mirror. She looked good. She was going to spend the morning in her father's box watching the ponygirls race with Drabik. Hopefully, she could get him to come back to her tent right after the pony parade. The slut's tongue had been good, but she needed a cock!

CHAPTER TWO

It was a little after eight o'clock and the ponygirl parade was about to begin. Jake was sitting in the grandstands with his new found lady friend, Tanya. You might say that they had become quite attached to one another. Jake went to scratch an itch on his cheek and a feminine, but quite strong, hand came up with it. He smiled and apologized.

When Tanya had awoken that morning, she had insisted that he climb back into bed with her. It was a demand that he was more than ready to give in to. They had torn off a quick one, both of them screaming their orgasms into the small room of the trailer. When they were done, Jake made his apologies and dressed.

"I've really got to get going," Jake said. "It's been great." He wondered if he should promise to call like he used to do in the old days when he lived somewhere that had telephones. He had met the pretty girl at Burnham's party the night before. He had had a little too much gin and ale and had danced the night away with the Kalikastani native. He had awoken in her bed, not sure of who she was or where he was. It had taken a while to figure it out. He had just been trying to slip out of the girl's trailer unnoticed when she woke up and challenged him to another bout of sexual bliss.

Tanya was up too. "Please wait and I'll come out with you," she said, a soft smile on her face. Jake felt it was the least he could do after the enjoyable interchange he had

had with her. She grabbed some clothes from her dresser and ran out of the bedroom.

The blond haired girl emerged from the bathroom looking remarkably refreshed. Her short hair had been combed and she was wearing a tight pair of blue jeans and a light green t-shirt. She had white Reeboks on her feet with pink laces. She smiled and grabbed Jake's arm as they stepped out of the trailer.

To Jake's surprise, a trio of men was sitting around a campfire eating breakfast. Two of the men were younger, about Tanya's age, and the other man looked like he could be her father. The way that he smiled when he looked at her indicated to him that the man definitely was.

"What did the cat drag home, Tanya?" he called out to her in Russian, rising to his feet. The other men did too. Jake felt one of those fight or flight issues coming on.

"Speak English, Papa," Tanya said. "This is my future husband."

The men all laughed. Jake didn't know whether to laugh or not.

"And what is this husband's name?" the father asked.

"His name is Jake Barnes, Papa," Tanya replied merrily. "He's an American who works with the infamous Mr. Burnham. We're going to spend the day together."

"Oh, I couldn't…." Jake started to say. He wanted to get out of there as soon as possible.

Just then he felt a cold click on his arm. He looked down. Tanya had slipped a handcuff over his wrist. She clicked the other end on hers. She tossed the key to her father.

"Papa, please hold on to this for me. I don't want this one to get away." She was laughing as were all the men.

"If I were you, Mr. Barnes, I'd be getting the wedding announcements out very soon. Tanya always gets what she wants."

Jake was too startled to reply. How was he going to go around all day wearing this girl on his arm? And getting married to anyone, even as good a fuck as Tanya, was the last thing that he wanted. It was a good thing he was leaving in a couple of days.

The older man stepped forward. He had short, curly, salt and pepper hair, and was wearing a dark brown corduroy shirt. He had black work pants on and heavy boots. He reached out his hand as he approached the couple.

"My name is Vassily Strelnikov," he said, smiling. Fortunately, Jake's left hand was secured to Tanya's. He held out his right. "Pleased to meet you," he said weakly.

"So," Vassily said as the two men measured each other's cujones, "did you like fucking my daughter?"

Jake was taken aback. The man's eyes were strong, but he detected an element of merriment in them. Should he say yes or no, he thought, panicked. Social situations were not Jake's forte.

The big man laughed, a hearty, friendly laugh. "Don't be embarrassed my American friend. Tanya is a liberated woman as we are all liberated men. If my sons here, Boris and Ivan, can fuck all the slave girls they want, then Tanya must have her rights as well. It's a good thing we don't have little slave boys running around or poor Tanya would go wild."

"Oh, er," Jake started to say. The man still had hold of his hand.

"It's the same arrangement I have with her mother, Helena. If I didn't let her have her way, one morning I'd wake up with my balls in a jar."

The boys and father laughed, but Jake could see the truth of the statement in their eyes.

"I've got to get over to the grandstands," Jake mumbled, his hand finally released by the father, if not the daughter.

"We're all going there too," Tanya said. "Papa and the boys will sit in the owner's booth, but I'm going to sit with you."

"Owner's booth," Jake repeated stupidly.

"Oh, yes, Papa's cabriolet team made it into the tournament. It's our first time."

"Well, congratulations, Mr. Strelnikov," Jake said, surprised. "I hope you do well. Do you have a good driver?"

"Of course we do!" Tanya exclaimed. "It's my mother!"

"You're mother?" Jake replied, incredulous. He wasn't aware that equal opportunity had spread its reach to this remote, backwards country.

Vassily laughed again. "She's a hell of a driver and she knows how to handle a ponygirl," he said. "I had to take it up with the Rules Committee. When I pointed out that nowhere in the rules did it say that drivers had to be men, they relented."

Jake was overwhelmed by this morning's developments. Well, if the old man didn't mind him fucking his daughter, then, maybe everything would turn out all right. But there was still the issue of him wearing her for the whole day. What would he say to Irkut? And people were bound to stare. But since the father had the key, it looked like he was stuck. He cast his eyes on the pleasing young woman. There was something about her that really turned him on. He wondered if he could get her to come back to his trailer with him after the first round of races.

"Come on, Mr. Barnes," Tanya said teasingly. "We're going to miss the parade."

And that was why the girl's hand lifted when he went to scratch his cheek. Irkut, the Burnham estate's head ponygirl trainer, had met him at the estate box in the grandstands. Burnham, who once he had learned the delights of living in a country where slave girls were ubiquitous, and tall, sleek, former women could be owned and forced to run before a cart, had relocated his business empire here. He had purchased seats for a good number of his executives and they were already raucously drinking the local ale, frat boy style.

"After the parade, we can find some better seats," Jake whispered to Tanya. She smiled back.

"Or we could find a nice bed," she said. "I want to suck your cock some more, my big American boyfriend," she said, laughing.

It was odd that after so much sexual licentiousness, the ubiquitous, available, naked slave girls, the tall, broad shouldered, faceless and anonymous ponygirls ready for fucking any time day or night, that Jake remained somewhat prudish about his sexual life. It embarrassed him to have a free, independent and self willed woman express so blatantly her sexual desires. But it was exciting too, like ice cream before dinner, sinful and pleasurable.

He turned to look at her and saw her frank, open stare in return. "Why not," he told her.

The ponies were just beginning to enter the track. In the background was playing a scratchy recording of what served as the Kalikastani National Anthem and most of the people in the stands rose to their feet in deference to it. It had no words as far as Jake knew, but every state needed to have the trappings of national pride and Kalikastan, a nation overrun by Russians and now being bought up by the Americans, was no exception.

By the time that the anthem ended, the ponies had reached the grandstands. They were led by the show ponies, a first for this year and a recognition of their growing acceptance as a sport. The dainty ponies kicked their slender knees high in time to a jaunty, military tune played over the loudspeakers, and the pastel plumes matching their pastel hoods shook and waved in the wind. Behind each team walked their trainers holding long reins connected to bits in the ponies' mouths. Jake saw the lavender two pony team that he had so enjoyed watching with Irkut the day before. He pointed them out to Tanya.

"Oh, they're so pretty!" Tanya exclaimed. "You see that foursome with the sea green hoods? I've been working with them as a kind of apprentice trainer. I'm going to get my own pair over the winter and my mother is going to help me train them."

Jake was astounded that such a sweet, young girl would be associated with anything as harsh as training ponygirls. You had to be hard and cruel and ready with a whip. The enslavement of women did not seem to fit well with Tanya's fierce streak of independence. Hers was a strange breed of feminism. On the other hand, if men had the right to exploit women's bodies for their own unrestrained pleasures, why not women too?

Once the show ponies had passed, the cabriolets were next. The six pony teams, harnessed in three pairs before each carriage, kicked and pranced in unison when they came opposite the grandstands. The crowd, having politely applauded the show ponies came alive once the racing ponies came into view.

"There's my mother!" Tanya screamed. She stood and waved. "Mama! Mama! Over here!" She swished her extended arms back and forth, bringing Jake's left arm with her. Jake saw the driver, a heavyset, grey haired matron, wearing blue, red and green colors, move her head to the side for just one moment and smile. Her six ponies cantered beautifully as they passed. To Jake it looked like she handled them as well as any of the men.

When he was able to sit back down, he asked the slender man next to him, "What do you think about women drivers, Irkut?"

The older man looked pensive for a moment. "I've always said that handling a ponygirl was more a matter of will than brawn, so I don't see why a woman couldn't do as well as a man. Of course, to drive them well, especially the larger teams, you need strength, especially in the hands. With two ponies at the front, it's not too bad. I don't know about the landau teams though. To pull on three sets of reins at once requires strength and agility. The agility is there, I'm sure, but the strength, well time will tell, I guess. Sooner or later a woman will try her hand at it, if you pardon the pun. I'll reserve judgment until then."

"So you don't oppose it on account of any principle?" Jake inquired.

"No," Irkut answered firmly. "The teams work hard and must go through a terrible transformation to become ponygirls. They deserve the best drivers be they men or women. The thing to avoid though is to permit the sport to be taken over by dilettantes. I understand that the Racing Commission is considering licensing of drivers and a mandatory apprentice period. It might be a good idea."

Jake turned back to the parade. Ten teams of six ponies each passed the spectators and were followed by the three pony troikas and then the four pony broughams. He sat up with particular attention to watch the landaus, which were next. Aside from the sulkies in which he had more than an academic interest, the long, gaudily painted, gold trimmed carriages, each bearing a driver and a formally attired passenger, were Jake's favorites. He was constantly amazed at how well coordinated the nine pony teams were. In precise rows of three each, the ponies lifted and lowered their black booted feet in perfect harmony. Their large breasts fluttered and jumped and their plumes waved proudly in the early morning breeze. Like all of the other racing ponies, their bodies were muscular but sleek, only more so.

It was a conceit of the sport that the better teams strove for aesthetics as well as speed. One team had ponies who all sported long, graceful, blond tails, another, black. One team matched alternated rows of light skinned, pale, Northern European ponies with a middle row of darker hued Mediterranean types. This year, Jake had been told by Irkut, there was the first all black landau team, imported from the urban streets of America and Europe. He watched them coming up now in the parade. Their coal black, shiny bodies were perfect and alluring. They wore dark maroon hoods and black plumes. Jake felt a surge of lust as he watched their breasts flow as they cantered before the stands. On their bellies, above their hairless slits, they were stenciled with fierce looking green and red dragons. Atop the landau driver's seat sat a tall, broad shouldered black man. He was uniformed in a jaunty hat with a sort of New Orleans flair. In the passenger seat sat a large, dark hued fellow sporting a top hat and tails. He waved back to the crowd happily as they passed. Jake watched through a pair of binoculars that Irkut had graciously brought for him. Tanya begged to use them too and, after a good long look at the enticing intimacies of the black ponies, Jake handed the glasses to her.

"They're perfect!" Tanya shouted. "I'd like to get a pretty black pair of show ponies to work with. I love their skin, its so rich and flavorful looking."

Jake agreed.

After the landaus came the yearlings. A yearling was a pony new to her bit and in her first racing season. Jake had become schooled enough in the sport to notice that the first run teams were just a little less well coordinated than the older, more experienced ones. They seemed just a little more put off by the cheering crowds and the gawking onlookers. Compared to the landau teams, most of them seemed slender. Irkut had told him that during the winter months, when they would be housed in the large barns near the capital with indoor, heated tracks, the trainers there would work on beefing them up with special diets and lots of hard work. Some of them though would be groomed as sulky runners and kept lean.

Jake was constantly surprised at how well organized and almost scientific the sport of ponygirl racing had become. When he had first heard of it back in the early spring, he had imagined the sometimes plump, pale skinned women that you tended to see on grainy videos on the Internet, wearing bells and long skeins of strait hair shoved up their asses. He wondered what those ladies would make of the real thing, hooded and faceless, their human qualities all but erased for all time. This was no fetish for weekenders.

After the yearlings came the sulkies. The 1500 meter ponies were first. Chocolate was third in line. He watched through the binoculars as she raised and lowered her knees in perfect time with the gay, martial music that was being played. Tanya sensed that he had a special interest in her.

"I helped recruit her," was all Jake could tell her, especially with Irkut present.

"Oh, I've heard all about her,' Tanya returned. "She looks so pretty. How does she fuck?"

Jake, taken aback by the young girl's bluntness, turned a little red in the face.

"Oh, he's blushing!" Tanya exclaimed. "Don't you think I know you fuck ponygirls?" she asked. "When we're married, I'll let you do it just as long as you let me too."

"When you're married?' Irkut asked, laughing. "When did all this come about?"

"Oh, last night," Tanya replied. "I decided when he had his face buried in my quim. I said 'I can't let a man who eats pussy this good get away!'"

Irkut laughed again. He patted Jake on the back. "A true tribute, my friend!"

Jake turned his attention back to Chocolate. How was she holding up, he wondered. She looked good and strong. He wanted desperately to give her words of encouragement. He had already decided that, win or lose, the escape operation was on. He would bring Jackie out by hook or by crook if it was the last thing he did.

Finally, last of all, came the 3000 meter sulkies. Lightning was first as befitted her top seed. She pranced beautifully. He hoped that her foot injury, which everyone was talking about, would hold up. It was ironic that her redeemer from a life of abject servitude was a mere 100 yards ahead of her and she didn't even know it. In fact, the two ponies could pass right next to each other and both would be oblivious to the other's identity. If only he could get word to her. It was doubly ironic that she would probably be running her heart out when it came to the match race, ignorant of the fact that with each strenuous stride she was advancing her own doom. There was no way Jake could snatch her if she won the race. Security would be too tight.

As the sulkies finished passing by, the heavyweight ponies that had run the day before brought up the rear. They were dragging their sleds behind them, packing down the track where the pony parade had passed by. Czarina, the former Maureen Donaldson, led them all, sporting her gold medal affixed to her collar. There was a round of merry applause for them from the onlookers. To Jake, her demeanor seemed especially proud, her shoulders straight, her head held up high. Andreyev, her youthful driver, rode her sled dressed in his racing clothes. He waved happily to the crowd.

"Okay," Tanya said as the last of the big ponies went by, "let's go and fuck."

* * * * * * * * * * * * *

Up in the owner's booth, Drabik was seething. Anya was being a royal pain in the ass. She kept looking at him lasciviously and dropping double entendres dripping with sexual innuendo. Her father, Axmail, was right there with them. How the old man could not know by know that he was fucking his daughter was beyond him.

Anya was sitting just to Grobgy's right and he was on the man's left. He had to have heard every word that she spoke. Drabik had to admit that she was especially alluring this morning. Her obvious anger at him made his prick rise.

Not that he hadn't had his fun the night before, ignoring Anya's slave girl's entreaties that he go to her mistress's tent. He had spent the night fucking one of Grobgy's pretty, little slave girls. He had made her whine with pain as he abused her. This morning he had fucked her ass brutally and then thrown her out. Every waking moment of his life now seemed to be filled with anger.

Redemption was only days away. He had plans to overthrow his criminal master, plans that had been long in preparation. His move would be made as soon as the tournament was over. He had received the go ahead from the National Commission after the payment of a heavy bribe. The money, ironically, was Grobgy's, stolen by Drabik from a number of Grobgy's drug dealers. None of them lived to tell the tale since that would have revealed Drabik's plot and brought about his doom. It was Grobgy's mindless striking out at other criminal organizations he believed responsible for the thefts that had gotten him in trouble with the Commission. It was funny how things were working out.

Drabik imagined that the tension of his gamble for the right to rule Grobgy's criminal empire was getting to him. And so was the fear that Lightning would be lost by the old man's foolish wager with the American billionaire, Michael Burnham. But Grobgy, who had refused Burnham's efforts to buy the ponygirl champion, could not resist a good gamble. Lightning was the master of the 3000 meter after all. And it would be a grand thing to own the two fastest ponygirls in the country, Lightning and Chocolate.

Naked slave girls whirled around the owner's booth delivering drinks and food to the wealthy patrons of the sport. Here and there one was captured by one of the men and made to perform some sexual service. He knew that the girls greased themselves up on occasions like this. It was hard to be sexually ready all the time especially when you were frantically running around delivering food and beverages. Grobgy had one between his knees now, sucking his prick. She had auburn hair and tiny breasts. She was child like, only a little over 5' tall, and skinny. Drabik wondered who had picked her out for service in Kalikastan and where she was from. Someone, somewhere, had a penchant for little girls and had satisfied that whim by importing a doll like, little woman.

The use of females under eighteen was frowned upon. First of all, the kidnapping of children went far beyond the pale as far as the authorities in foreign lands were concerned, who were often paid to look the other way when mature girls were harvested. There was also local public opinion to be considered. There were those, even in Kalikastan, that thought that the forcible indenture of beautiful women was virtually medieval, and the use of children would be grist for their mill. It was a small minority, and not very vocal since, after all, Kalikastan was not a democracy. Secret police were everywhere enforcing the National Commission's right to power. There were prisons and executions even in Kalikastan. Thirdly, having broken almost every other basic taboo of civilized society, there had to be some places that they just would not go.

Drabik brightened up when Lightning came prancing by. He took out his binoculars and had a good look at her. "Soon she will be mine," he thought. His heart began to pound with the fever of his desire for her as she pranced her way across the grandstand. He had never had such an obsession with a female before. He could normally take them or leave them, but mostly take them. In Afghanistan, when he commanded a battalion of motherfuckers, he had gotten a taste for forcing women to his will. When he began to work in the Russian underworld after the dissolution of the Soviet empire and his release as redundant from the Red Army, he fucked many pretty, young girls who had been 'persuaded' to work as whores for his boss. Once Grobgy had his hooks in them, they became virtual slaves. Even his fucking of Anya was a combination of convenience and the thrill that it gave him to pork the old man's daughter.

Anya was watching her lover intently. She saw how he perked up when Lightning came marching by. She had been taunting him the whole time during the parade, hoping to provoke him into fucking her, even if just to shut her up. She had decided that if his reticence to lend her his long, thick cock continued she would let her father know what he had been doing. The old man would kill him for sure like he had the others. Dropping hints in front of her father as to their relationship was her way of letting Drabik know that he skated on thin ice. No one dumped her, not even the notorious killer, Anton Drabik.

Her father was still receiving the oral attentions of the little slave girl. Anya was disgusted that he had so little consideration as to get a blowjob right in front of her. She had no desire to see his greasy cock displayed. She had seen plenty of men fucking both slaves and ponygirls. But to watch her own father was beyond the pale. She got up to leave. "I'll see you later, Father," she said coldly. She strode quickly to the back of the booth and stepped out into the hallway.

Drabik saw the spoiled and dangerous, jaded, young woman leave. He decided that it was worth his while to placate her wrath. She had to go when Grobgy did, that was for sure, but for now, she could ruin all of his plans by giving her father an excuse to shoot him on the spot.

"I've got to go and check on out brougham team," he told his boss. Axmail's head was leaning back and his eyes were closed.

"Of course," he muttered.

Drabik got up from his chair and hurried off. He caught up with Anya just as she was about to enter the stairwell to go downstairs to the public areas. "Anya!" he called. "Wait for me!"

The tall, dark haired beauty spun around. "What for, Anton?" she said coldly. "Don't you want to make sure that your pony lover is all right? I heard she had a little accident."

Drabik ignored the barb. "Come here," he said, as he pulled her into the stairway used by the slave girls to run up and down to the kitchen. When the double swinging doors closed behind them, he pushed her up against the wall, grabbed her face and put his lips to hers. Just like in the movies, Anya, after a dulsatory effort to fight him off, opened her lips and took his hot tongue inside.

They kissed long and passionately. The occasional slave girl came running up or down the stairs past them. When they broke, Anya was out of breath. "Oh, Anton," she said. "I've missed you. Why didn't you come to me last night?"

"Shut up," Drabik said. He grabbed her by the shoulders and spun her around. He ran his hands around her chest and seized her heavy breasts and pushed his body up against her.

"Since when do ponygirls get to make demands on their masters?" he asked her. "You're my little ponygirl aren't you?"

He was referring to the little games they played when isolated in the country inn where they had their trysts. It was about 20 miles from the Grobgy estate and they thought that they were safe there. They didn't know that Grobgy had sussed them out.

Anya felt a surge of lust run through her as she was reminded of their wildly passionate interludes. He would dress her up in ponygirl regalia and fuck her as if she were one of the dehumanized creatures. It drove her crazy with need. As his hands worried her full, firm breasts, she felt her blood rising.

"Oh, Anton," she said, "not here."

"You'll fuck me anywhere I say, Anya," Drabik replied, "like the slut that you are."

He intensified his grasp on her twin peaks and Anya moaned as the pain and pleasure mixed. His cock was hard as a rock. Leaning over, he began to kiss her bare neck. Anya moaned with pleasure and rubbed her ass against his cock wantonly. Her hands were pressed up against the cool, concrete wall of the stairwell.

"Please, Anton," she hissed through belabored breath. It was not clear if she was begging him to stop or to keep going. Perhaps she didn't know herself.

Drabik eased his purchase on her breasts and ran his hands down her thighs and over her hips. He grabbed the skirt of her dress and began to pull it up.

'No, Anton," Anya moaned, "please don't." But she made no effort to stop him. When her skirt's hem was brought waist high, Drabik tucked it between his belly and her back and caressed her long, bare, supple thighs. Her skin was hot and her body trembled as it recorded his fevered touch. Anya wore no panties and his still concealed cock pressed up against her bare ass.

"I'm going to fuck you, Anya," Drabik told her. "I'm going to fuck you like a slave girl. That's what you are: my little slave girl. You should be running around naked with a collar and leather bracelets on, Anya. I should have your name tattooed on your chest and my mark put on your belly. Would you like that Anya, to be my slave girl?"

"Nooooooo," Anya moaned, but her body said yes.

Drabik moved his hips back slightly so that he could free his cock from its enclosure. He lowered his zipper and fished it out. He pulled her hips away from the wall and then pushed down on her back. He kicked her black booted legs apart and began to rub her revealed pussy. It was hot and wet with anticipation of his prick.

"You're a slut, Anya," Drabik told her. "You melt whenever you think of a cock in one of your holes. When the tournament's over, I'm going to take you to our special place and fuck you like a ponygirl. I'll put you in a ponygirl collar," he told her as he rubbed her puss, "and fill your slutty mouth with a big, thick gag. I'll hood you and lock your arms behind your back like a real ponygirl. And then I'll fuck you for hours. Would you like that, Anya?"

"Yessssssss," Anna moaned. "Fuck me like a ponygirl, Anton! Be my master!"

Drabik removed his hand from between the tall, beautiful woman's thighs, and replaced it with his rampant cock. "Here comes my prick, whore," he told her. "Take it up your hungry snatch."

Pressing his hips forward, Drabik slid his cock into the lubricated gash. Anya sighed deeply as she felt herself possessed. Her torso was bent over and she held herself up with her hands against the wall. Her legs were splayed wide apart and her back was arched. "Oh, god!" she moaned as the killer's motions began. "Oh, fuck me Anton! Fuck me!"

The slave girls continued to pass to and fro. Some of them tittered quietly when they saw the free woman being treated as a slave girl would. Others, fearful of the couple's wrath if they made any sign that they saw them rutting like beasts in the stairwell, hurried by. Slave girls quickly become expert at not being noticed and holding in their emotions. A small gaggle of them had gathered at the bottom of the stairs and were giggling as they listened to the free woman beg for the man's cock.

The muscular ponygirl trainer sawed his hot piece rapidly back and forth inside Anya's needy canal. She moaned and sighed as he fucked her. His hands found their way back to her ample breasts and squeezed them hard. The bright, white blouse that she wore was open down past the divide between her full breasts. Drabik insinuated his hands inside and popped the next two buttons open. Anya almost always wore a bra. She was aware that her 22 year old breasts, firm and upstanding as they were, would be around her knees when she was thirty-five if she did not take care of them. Today she wore a flimsy, lacey thing that gave them just enough support so that they resisted gravity's pull. Drabik easily pulled the cups upwards and over the breasts, freeing the delicious orbs.

The young woman groaned as Drabik's hot, rough hands took possession of her bare bosom. He pulled at her thick nipples as he fucked her, pinching them hard.

"You like it when I hurt you, don't you, Anya?" Drabik taunted her. His breath was deep and heavy as his juices began to rise. The girl was in no state to answer him as she started a staccato groan.

Two naked slave girls entered the stairwell through the swinging doors gossiping loudly about this thing or other. Anya's moan startled them. She was coming now and had lost any of the little restraint that she had left. "Ohhhhhhhhh! Ohhhhhhhhhh!" she called out. The two slave girls jumped when they heard her voice, looked over and then scurried down the stairs. They were met at the bottom by a group of nattering, naked compatriots. A man came out of the kitchen and saw the slave girls milling around.

"Let's get back to work!" he yelled. "Unless you want to get a whipping!"

The girls dashed off as if shot from cannons. The man watched them stream into the kitchen. He then heard the grunts and moans of the coupling duo at the top of the stairs and smiled. No slave girl he knew would be calling her master's name, "Anton! Anton! Oh my god, Anton!" He laughed and went back into the kitchen.

Anya's hole began a new series of convulsions when Drabik's prick began its dance of joy within her. The hot, thick discharge splashed against the walls of her womb. "Auuuuuuugh! Auuuuuuuugh!" she called out lustfully as she came. His hands had moved to her hips, holding her steady as he pumped in and out of her cunt. Her breasts were swinging wildly beneath her chest, put in motion by the slamming of her lover's hips against her ass. Drabik just grunted his pleasure.

Once his balls had emptied themselves in Anya's shuddering crevasse, Drabik slowed his hips' thrusts until he reached a stop. Both he and Anya were breathing heavily, trying to recover their equilibrium. Drabik's returned first and he slipped his softened meat from the panting, bent over, young woman's slit, letting her black skirt fall back into place.

"I'll see you later, Anya," he told her, slapping her ass fiercely. "Remember, we have a date for three days from now."

He walked out through the double swinging doors. Anya was still propped up against the wall. When she heard Drabik leave, she murmured, "Anton," and straightened herself up. Her bra was up over her loosely hanging tits. A slave girl was coming up the stairs with a tray of food and stopped in shock when she saw the young woman in her dishabille.

"What are you looking at?" Anya screamed at her. "Get going or I'll have your skin peeled from your stupid face!"

The girl took off like a shot. Anya's temper cooled as her cunt remembered her just recent, round fucking and her mind savored the thought of her rendezvous with her father's killer three days hence. She tucked her mammaries back into their homes and straightened her skirt. Her blood was still up. Since Natalie was gone, she would have to pick another one of her father's slave girls to be her minion. That was okay. Anya always started her body slaves off with a good whipping and it was just what she was in the mood for.

CHAPTER THREE

Chocolate's first heat was at 10:30. Jake and Tanya made it back to the grandstands with a few miniutes to spare. Irkut had some friends with a box some distance from the Burnham box and they met him there so as to avoid the necessity of putting up with the schoolboy jokes and pranks from the American executives.

Tanya's mother's team had a tough match against a higher seed. She lost gallantly, to Tanya's disappointment, by not much more than a head. She would be placed against a team closer to her own abilities for her next match. Hopefully, she would go home with at least one victory. Not bad for a new team in its first tournament appearance.

The brown skinned pony did well in her first run, easily beating a pony with a lower seed. Lightning also had an easy race. Chocolate's next race, against the eighth seed pony, was supposed to be cakewalk as well. It turned out to be anything but.

The lovers grabbed a bite to eat from one of the vendors and killed time by walking through the exhibits and sideshows of the fair. The landau team with the nine coal black ponies was running at 12:30 and Chocolate was scheduled for her second match at 12:45. They made it back to the grandstand just in time to see the black ponies take off.

There was a great deal of room for variation in outcome in the landau races. With a single pony race, there were limited things that could go wrong. The driver only had to consider the morale and readiness of one pony, not nine. With the landaus there were so many variables that it would have been a misnomer to describe any as having a lock on the championship.

The black landau team was running against a team with blue and silver hoods. Jake enjoyed watching the coal black ponies in action. Their muscles seemed to ripple and flow over them. In the ¼ turn in the second 1500 meter lap, the blue and silver team, which had been leading, just seemed to lose its edge. The black skinned ponies quickly took and kept the lead until the very end. As the teams crossed the finish line, Irkut pointed out to Jake why the change in fortunes had occurred. He could see that the pony on the right end in the second row of the blue and silver team was limping. Apparently, she had pulled a muscle during the race. It was bad luck, but that was the way things went.

There was a four pony brougham match after that. It was one of Grobgy's teams, with blue and gold hoods. They defeated the other team handily.

Chocolate's second race was next. She was running against a pony that had done fairly well in the beginning of the season but whose fortunes had fallen off towards the end. It kind of cruised into the tournament based on its first half record. Irkut, who was a master at all of these things, pointed out in the racing program how its times had steadily fallen off. He was confident that Chocolate would do well.

The two ponies lined up. Chocolate's black and gold head bobbed anxiously while waiting for the starting gun. The other pony, with colors of red and green, stood poised next to her. Chocolate, as the favorite, had the outside rail. The starting gun sounded and they went off.

The red and blue pony took off like a shot. The 1500 race was a sprint, but you still had to leave something for the last 500 meters or so. This pony seemed like it was going to zoom wire to wire.

"Look how fast she's going," Tanya said. "She can't keep up that pace. What's she doing?"

"You mean 'What's her driver doing?'" Irkut replied. He was watching the pony, who had taken a three length lead on Chocolate before the quarter pole, through his binoculars. "The way she's sweating," he added, "she'll be out of gas very soon."

Another pair of eyes was watching the race with intense interest. Up in the owner's booth, Anton Drabik also had binoculars to his eyes. He knew the driver of the red and blue hooded pony very well. It was clear he had no shot at a medal. So why not walk away with a little cash.

There was more than one way to insure that the match race between Chocolate and Lightning never took place. Lightning's injury seemed to have been overcome, which meant that she still had a good chance to win her division. But if Chocolate didn't win hers too, there would be no match race. Injuries on the race rack were common, especially in the highly charged atmosphere of the tournament. And a little juice could make the chance of an accident more likely.

Chocolate had gained on the other pony steadily. By the midway pole, she was moving to pass her. Suddenly, the red and blue pony veered to the right. She ran directly across Chocolate's path. Chocolate tried to pull up to avoid a collision, but it was too late. Her left leg banged against the spinning wheel of the other cart and she went down.

The entire audience rose to their feet and moaned. Chocolate was a sentimental favorite with the crowd. It would be a shame for her to lose the tournament because of an injury.

The red and blue pony kept on going. Chocolate pulled herself up off the dirt track and tried to follow. She made about three steps and she collapsed again.

Giorgi had been pleased with the other pony driver's strategy. He knew that he could not maintain that pace through the whole 1500 meters. Giorgi ran his pony at just enough speed to catch the other one during the far stretch and then cruise to victory, probably with a lead of six or seven lengths, maybe more. He could have caught the other pony earlier and ran her into the ground, but Chocolate had at least one more match today and more tomorrow. He wanted to conserve her strength for when she really needed it. The second seed pony had run on the southern circuit this year and Chocolate had not seen her yet. She was young and fast and set a track record in her last race before the Tournament. She would be Chocolate's toughest competitor and probably the other finalist two days hence. Lightning had to race her either later today or tomorrow morning.

Seeing the red and blue pony make its lunge to the right, he had tried to guide Chocolate away from her by having her turn right as well. But the other pony kept coming and coming. It was like she was being deliberately steered into Chocolate's path.

When he saw Chocolate go down, his heart fell. If she got up quickly, there was still a chance to win the race. The rules prevented him from leaving his seat to help her. Once he got off the seat of the sulky, they would be disqualified.

His heart rejoiced when she got to her feet. "Go! Go!" he yelled at her, cracking the whip, not so it struck her, but so it made a distinctly encouraging sound just behind her. She took three steps and fell once more.

Frantic, Giorgi leapt from his seat. All thoughts of avoiding a forfeit were out of his head. It looked like Chocolate might be out of the tournament altogether.

Jake and Irkut took off to go down to the field level at the same time. Jake, however, being manacled to Tanya, had a little harder time doing it. He looked at the girl who signaled him that she understood and the two of them flew down the stairs together.

Jake had a pass denoting him as part of the management team of the Burnham entries. The security guard down at the field level saw it and then looked askance at the young woman affixed to him. He shrugged his shoulders and let them both through.

When they reached Chocolate and her driver, He was kneeling over her, rubbing her leg.

"That motherfucker!" Giorgi was ranting. "I'll kill that bastard! I'll kill him!"

Jake looked up at the tote board and saw the inquiry light on meaning that the officials were looking at the race. That the other pony had won it was not in doubt in the sense that she had crossed the finish line and Chocolate had not. But a foul had clearly occurred and if she was awarded the race, there would surely be a protest from Burnham.

Chocolate was lying in the dirt of the track, moaning. Her injured leg was lying flat and her undamaged one was bent at the knee and swaying back and forth. Giorgi had released all of her straps to the sulky.

Jake heard the sound of someone heavyset coming up the track towards them and turned to see Burnham, red as a beet, approaching at a trot. He had his security guard, Nicholai Borodin, with him.

"How is she? How is she?" he yelled. "Is her leg broken? Can she still run?"

Irkut turned towards him. "I don't know. I'll let you know what I think in a minute." He tapped Giorgi on the shoulder. "Move away friend and let me have a look at her."

Giorgi reluctantly stepped aside. "He did that on purpose, that bastard! I'll kill him for this!"

Irkut placed his hands on Chocolate's thigh and began a careful massage. Chocolate moaned, but she did not jump. It was a good sign.

"I don't think anything's broken, but her muscle has suffered a severe bruise. She needs to be treated right away." He stood and signaled to the security officials to get the first aid cart out on the track. A few moments later, a cart pulled by two tall, broad shouldered, brown tailed, naked, work ponygirls came trundling towards them. They had a flatbed behind them for transporting injured racers.

When the cart arrived, Jake, Irkut and one of the track officials picked Chocolate up from the track and put her on it. Just then the crowd started an audible murmur and then a round of applause. Jake looked up at the tote board and saw that the race had been awarded to Chocolate. Well that was good at least. But if she could no longer run then everything was done. Maddy the ponygirl would remain so, perhaps forever. All of his work, all of the evil that he had permitted and even encouraged to exist in his drive to free the ponygirl would not be offset by any 'greater good'.

"Take her to the aid station and get some ice on that thigh right away," the official said. The driver of the first aid cart turned his ponies and they trotted off quickly. Burnham, Jake, Irkut, Giorgi and Tanya, of course, followed closely.

Burnham was steaming mad. "Why the fuck did that driver do that?" he asked no one in particular.

Irkut answered him. "He was undoubtedly paid by someone in the Grobgy camp who does not want your pony to race Lightning in a match race," he said. "I know this driver for a long time. He's a scoundrel and a fool. He should have been run off a long time ago, but he drives cheaply and has experience. With the expansion in the sport the last few years, experienced drivers are not easy to come by."

The group was walking briskly to get to the aid station as soon as possible. Burnham looked at Jake and then at Tanya. "Who the fuck is this?" he barked angrily.

"She's a friend of mine, Mr. Burnham," Jake answered.

"Well, get rid of her, we have to talk!" Burnham retorted.

"I can't," Jake replied, lifting his manacled left arm. Burnham took a look at it and stopped dead in his tracks.

"Is this some kind of a fucking joke?" he asked petulantly. "Are we playing games here Jake?"

"No, Mr. Burnham," Jake said sheepishly.

"You know, you've been living over in my cottage, fucking all of my slave girls, drinking my booze these many months and doing nothing!" he yelled. "I don't pay you to shack up with local whores and have fun and games! What good are you to me, Jake? Why shouldn't I fire you right on the spot?"

Jake's ire was up too. Yes, he had been lax, even he admitted that. But Burnham knew why he had nothing to do but wait. He knew why Jake was here in the first place.

But he could say nothing in front of these others. All he could say was, "You know why, Mr. Burnham. Or have you forgotten?"

The look that Burnham gave was fit to kill him. "We'll talk about this later, Jake," Burnham said. He then turned and started walking again to the first aid tent.

Chocolate was there already and some of the men had placed her on one of the examining tables and strapped her in. The on staff physician was already looking at her thigh.

"I don't think it's broken," he said in Russian. "But it's going to be very sore for a while. I'd say she's finished."

"Speak English for Mr. Burnham," Irkut told him.

"I said that I don't think your pony can do any more racing in this tournament, Mr. Burnham," he said in English.

"We'll see about that," Burnham replied.

"I won't certify her as fit," the doctor replied. "If I say she's finished, she's finished, and that's all there is to it, Mr. Burnham. The Americans don't run this sport yet."

Burnham looked like he was about to murder the man. Irkut pushed him away. "Let me handle this, Mr. Burnham," he said. "You go take care of your business. I'll fill you in later."

Burnham, his face red as a rooster, turned and stormed off. His tough looking and inscrutable security chief went off with him. Irkut turned to the doctor. "Now Alexei, you don't have to make your decision today. Let's see how she does in the morning, okay?"

Alexei's visage softened. "For you, Irkut, not for that bastard."

"We need to talk, Alexei. Can you give us a few minutes alone?"

"Okay," he replied and walked off.

"First things first," Irkut said. "Chocolate has one more heat today if we're lucky. If there's two, we're screwed."

"How's that," Jake asked.

"Well, in order not to be disqualified from the tournament, Chocolate can have no forfeits. So, she has to be in her next race no matter what."

"She's in no condition to race!" Jake shot out. She may be Chocolate to them, but she was still Jackie to him. He didn't want her permanently maimed.

"She has to finish, that's all" Irkut said. "She can walk. If she loses, she loses. It's double elimination, remember. As long as there's no fourth race for her to run tonight, and she can recover before her first race in the morning, she'll be okay."

"But you heard the doctor," Jake pleaded. "He says she's finished."

"That's what he says now. We've got to get her iced up and then we'll see. If she's properly wrapped and rests the leg, maybe she'll be okay. I've seen ponies recover from worse injuries. She's got a lot of heart and I think that she can do it."

All of this was occurring right above Chocolate as she lay naked on the first aid table. There was no way that she wanted to give in. Oddly, if she was finished racing, her work was done and Jake could start the procedures necessary to get her home. Something inside her, though, wanted to complete the job she had come to Kalikastan to do, to give meaning to all of her suffering. If only she could talk. She gave a whimper from behind her bit. It was good to hear Jake's voice after all these many months, but she wanted to tell him to shut the fuck up and mind his own business. She had confidence in her trainer, like all athletes should. And she wanted to win, like all champions do. She had lost the All Chicago High School medal by two one hundredths of a second her junior year. By the time it came around again the next year, she was turning tricks in an apartment on the North Side. She had blown the opportunity to be a champion. She did not want to blow it again.

"Where's the team doctor?" Tanya inserted. She had remained remarkably quiet following Burnham's tirade. Men have been shot for less in Kalikastan than calling a free woman a whore.

Even though she had been manacled to his wrist the whole time, Jake had forgotten she was there.

"I'm sorry for what Burnham said," he told her. "He was way out of line."

"Oh, don't worry about that, Mr. Barnes," she said playfully. "I liked the way you described me as your friend. That's a good start."

Jake laughed. Why did he have to meet someone like Tanya just before he was going to leave Kalikastan forever, he thought. She was a great piece of ass and a delightful, interesting person, and not necessarily in that order either.

Irkut answered Tanya's question. "That fucking asshole is an incompetent jerk. I wouldn't have him touch Chocolate with a ten meter pole."

"Maybe we can get my mother's doctor," Tanya said. "She never travels without Dr. Kevsky."

"That's a plan," Irkut said. "Let's ice her up for now. I'll stay here and take care of her. You two go and get Dr. Kevsky."

Jake and Tanya scooted off towards the ponypark. Her mother's next heat was not until 3-ish. Like all complicated events, the scheduling of the heats was a little ambitious. Things like having a ponygirl down on the track and eating up a precious fifteen minutes of schedule time were not provided for. Two incidents and you were off half an hour.

They reached the ponypark quickly. Tanya knew exactly where they were going. They received a good number of stares as a result of the handcuffs, but they ignored it. When they entered her mother's encampment, the woman was walking down her line of naked, hooded ponies, dressed in her red, blue and green racing gear. She was testing their harnesses and giving hem encouraging caresses. Seeing her up close, Jake could see that she was a beautiful woman. Her short, curly hair was mostly gray, but her body was firm and she moved with agility. She was, perhaps, just a little too hefty for him, but she definitely had her attractions.

"Tanya," she said excitedly when she saw her daughter. "How delightful to see you! Come to wish me luck?"

"Yes, Mama," Tanya replied in English. "And something else too. I need to see Dr. Kevsky."

"Dr. Kevsky went on an errand and will be back in a second or two. What's up?"

"Well, this is my friend, Jake Barnes…" she started to say.

"I know all about him. I talked to your father a little while ago. He came to console me on my loss. So will it be a winter or spring wedding? I like winter weddings; you can bundle up so cozily in bed."

"We haven't decided yet, Mama," Tanya said.

"Well…" Jake started to say.

"Don't worry, Mr. Barnes," Helena remarked, smiling, "I know that you haven't had time to let it sink in yet. But you'll get used to the idea, I promise you. We need another man around to help fuck all the ponygirls." She laughed as she slapped the rump of one of her leads. "In fact, if we win the next race, you can come over and give a hand rewarding them, take a little load off of my husband and my boys. You can fuck Molly here," she said. She seized one of the pony's breasts in her large, powerful hand and squeezed it playfully. "And if we lose, you can come and watch me whip them." The well disciplined pony did not flinch an inch.

"Well, I…" Jake started to say.

"Oh, he's shy, Mama," Tanya said. "He'll be happy to fuck Molly just as long as he leaves some for me."

Jake was not used to being speechless. He was no social sophisticate, but usually he could get a word in edgewise. These people were going to think he was a dolt.

He had not remarked on it when he had seen Helena's ponies before, but they all had long, orange ponytails. Their skin was as pale as porcelain. Their naked breasts were uniformly large and their shoulders broad and powerful. Here and there a spread of butterscotch colored freckles were strewn across a chest. They looked like six Irish Amazons. Molly looked like she would be a delight to fuck. She had a high, plump, hairless slit. On her belly, and on all the other ponies', was the tattoo of a minx, its claws raised as if to strike. It was appropriate for ponies trained by a woman, Jake thought.

Two tall, thin beauties had strolled up from the encampment. They looked like both younger and older models of Tanya, only with lighter hair. The younger one was very pretty and the older had smooth, handsome features. "What a family," Jake thought.

"These are my sisters, Zoya and Lada," Tanya said. They were dressed in blue jeans, boots and blue, red and green colored t-shirts. "They help Mama out with her team," Tanya added. "Lada, that's the younger one, wants to be a driver someday. She's really good with the ponies, just enough love and just enough pain. Right, Lada?"

"He's handsome," Lada said, avoiding the question. She had sweet, young hips and small, teenager's breasts. Zoya was more well built. She had the look of a sexual predator on her face.

"Is he good in bed?" she asked sultrily.

Before Tanya had time to answer, a tall, lanky, blond woman entered the campground. She was wearing jodhpurs, tall, brown leather boots and a loose, well filled, white, cotton blouse. Her hair was long and her face thin and pleasing. She looked about thirty five or so.

"Oh, here's the doctor now," Tanya's mother said.

"Okay," Tanya said. "Now I don't have to tell my story twice. Dr. Kevsky, this is Jake Barnes."

"I know who he is," Dr Kevsky said, smiling warmly. "Nice to meet you, Mr. Barnes," she said, holding out her hand. Jake took it and gave it a firm but pleasant shake.

"My pleasure, Doctor," he said.

"Call me Svetlana," the physician responded. She turned back to Tanya, smiling. "So when's the wedding?"

"We don't know yet," Tanya replied.

"That is…" Jake started to say.

"Oh, there's no rush, Mr. Barnes," the doctor interrupted him. "Anytime before the spring racing season is okay." She laughed. And to Tanya, she said, "You'll have to let me know when I can have him. He looks like he knows his way around a pussy."

"Not for a while," Tanya said. "We've just met and we need to get to know each other better first."

"I see you've already grown attached to each other," Kevsky retorted, laughing again.

Jake had heard that joke already a couple of times. It was getting old. He looked at the bevy of beautiful women. There were four very attractive, naked slave girls scurrying around the campsite doing their chores. He wondered what kind of social group he was getting involved in. Were they all joking about a wedding or not? His cock gave a little turn as the thought of fucking the shapely, pleasant looking doctor. The sisters too. Too bad he would never get the chance.

"We need you Dr. Kevsky," Tanya said. "Jake's pony, Chocolate, has gone down with a leg injury. She was fouled by the other team. We need you to look at it and wrap it up so she can at least walk for now."

"So that's what the commotion was," Helena said. "We heard the noise of the crowd way out here."

"I'll get my bag." The doctor went back to the large trailer and entered it. While she was gone, Jake made some small talk with Tanya's mother. "You have a beautiful team of ponies," he told her. "Irish?"

"As the day is long," she returned, laughing. "There's Molly, Megan and Kelly," she said pointing to the row on the left, "and Jodie, Clair and Fiona," pointing to the row on the right. "It took me a while to get them all together, but I did it. This is their first year as a cabriolet team. Kelly and Fiona are new this season. The other four pulled a brougham for me since last year. But it's the cabriolet I wanted to drive. I just love its lines and the sight of six ponies pulling it." Helena's carriage was set low to the ground with a high seat for the diver. It was made out of finely polished oak and had bright, brass fittings. She had bedecked it in her team's colors. Her pennant, a black minx on a red, blue and green background was hoisted at its rear.

Dr. Kevsky came out of the trailer with her little black bag. Helena gave the group a nod and hopped up on to the driver's seat of the carriage. "Come on," she said, "I'll give you all a ride down to the track. The ponies could use the exercise."

Jake, Tanya and the doctor climbed into the passenger section of the coach. The seats were made of fine, brown leather and comfortably padded. The seats faced each other. Jake and Tanya took seats facing the driver and Dr. Kevsky sat opposite them. Jake wanted to get a good look at the Irish ponies in motion. Helena snapped the reins and called out a guttural "Heyyyyyyy-ya!" The ponies leapt into action. Jake enjoyed the view of the ponies' orange tails bobbing as they ran and the muscles of their haunches as they rippled. They trotted in perfect unison. He was amazed at the speed they could get up to towing the large rig. Alone and empty it probably weighed three or four hundred pounds. The people in it added at least another 500. Of course the carriage was well engineered with strong, light alloys and well greased bearings. Jake wondered what Irving, his tech guy, could do to improve it. But then, he thought, Irving won't be around to do it. None of them would be.

It took a little over three minutes to get down to the first aid station. Jake let the women get out first and then followed them. The ponies had barely broken a sweat. It was a tribute to the rigor of Helena's training of them. Jake envisioned the somewhat hefty, self assured woman bringing a whip to bear on the ponies' delicate flesh. He was sure that the harshness of ponygirl life was not assuaged by the fact that the ponies were under the sway and domination of women. Probably, he thought, the exact opposite was true. He had seen how some of the Kalikastani women treated slave girls. It wasn't pretty.

"Good luck, Mama," Tanya called out as Helena drove her team off towards the paddock where she would await her upcoming race. Jake seconded his encouragement. As the ponies carried the carriage away, he couldn't help but wonder what was on the minds of the beautiful, hooded creatures at times like these. The incongruity of the normalcy which surrounded the harsh deprivation of all their human rights was intense to him. How much more so it must be for the ponies? Their fate must seem nightmarish, he thought. Every morning, he imagined, they woke up and found themselves still in the same, terrible dream. He thought of the pony he had seen yesterday, Irina, condemned to spend the next five or six years producing milk from her breasts so that idle wastrels like him could drink it or suckle it out of her. Every day she must feel a little more of her brain slip away. What could be more nightmarish than that?

Tanya disturbed Jake's pensive mood by giving his wrist a little tug. "Don't worry," she said. "Mama will let you fuck Molly win or lose. Let's get inside the tent so Dr. Kevsky can see Chocolate."

When they arrived at the examining table, Irkut was sitting on its edge. Giorgi was sitting on a high backed chair that made him look like a toy. Chocolate's thigh was wrapped in flexible bandages. A large lump of crushed ice was wrapped up too and attached to her left leg. She was lying peacefully and Irkut was playing with her breasts.

"Hello, Dr Kevsky," Irkut said. "I didn't know that you were Helena's team doctor."

"Helena and I are very good friends," the doctor said. "It's the least I can do for her."

Jake had begun to suspect that they were more than friends. If Helena swung that way, she had good taste. He wondered, though about the five kids.

The doctor removed the bandages and ice and conducted her own hands on examination of the pony's thigh. She agreed with Irkut's initial diagnosis. "I can give her a shot to ease the swelling," Dr. Kevsky said. "Just before her heat, I'll wrap the leg really tight."

Giorgi had been silent for a long time. "What do you think, doctor," the small man asked nervously.

"In my view," the beautiful, blond doctor said, "a good, relaxing, night's rest will do her a world of good. If the swelling is kept down there's a good chance she will be able to run on it tomorrow. We'll have to see. She won't be 100%, and there will be pain."

"She's a good runner," Giorgi added to no one in particular. "She's got a big heart. If she can run, she'll do it."

"I think its best if we relax her a little bit now," the doctor continued. "I can see that she's all tense. Is there a shield gag? I'll like to take her bit out for now." Giorgi went off to ask one of the first aid attendants if he had one.

Alexi, the track physician had joined the small assembly once again. "Good afternoon, Dr. Kevsky," he interjected. "I'm glad to see the pony is in good hands."

"Good afternoon to you, doctor," the blond woman replied. "I was just about to relax her. The plan is to walk her through her next race and then, if she has no more races today, see how she is in the morning."

"That seems reasonable," the doctor replied.

"I don't get it," Jake said. "If she was injured from a foul on the track, isn't it unfair to expect her to be able to run? Shouldn't they cut her some slack?"

"That's not the way it works," Irkut replied. "If they altered the schedule for every pony that got hurt, they'd have to make the tournament a month and a half long. Even if a pony is injured from a foul, there's no exception. Either she runs or she forfeits."

"That just seems stupid," Jake continued. "It really plays into the hands of anyone who wants to destroy a pony's chances of winning the tournament."

"Until today, I am unaware of any intentional fouls being declared by the Commission in any tournament race. It's just not done. Whoever did this has really placed themselves outside of the rules. My guess is that sooner or later, the driver of the other pony will fess up. There are some very serious methods of persuasion that can be used. The Commission will get to the bottom of this, fast."

Jake had a moment of intuition. He doubted that the driver would survive the night. That's how he would have run the operation. Dead men tell no tales.

Giorgi had produced a shield gag for the pony. The doctor reached behind its head and unbuckled its bit, removing it. She then presented the much more comfortable shield gag to the pony's mouth. Chocolate took it without question.

After the doctor had installed the gag, she began to slide her delicate hands over Chocolate's torso. She seized her recumbent breasts and caressed them, pinching at the nipples. She leaned over and took one in her mouth, giving it a long, enflaming kiss. Chocolate gave out a moan and her hips shifted slightly on the padded examining table. Her right ankle had been chained to a ring at the base of the table and the doctor moved to chain off her left. When the pony's legs were spread apart, she slid her hands up her shins and over her thighs.

"I'd like to thin out the crowd here a little bit," Kevsky said. "I don't think I'll be able to get her to come with all these people milling around, not under these circumstances."

The men all nodded and began to move off.

"Not you, Jake," the doctor interjected. "I sensed a definite relaxation in her every time that you spoke. Why don't you stay?"

"Okay, Doctor," Jake replied.

The doctor turned back to her patient. She caressed her hooded head several times and then circled the pony's breasts with her hands. She began to massage them gently. Chocolate stirred slightly.

Since everything had been spoken in English, Chocolate had understood all that the people had said. It was strange to be talked about as if you weren't there or couldn't hear. It was strange to her to be handled by a woman who was not a slave girl. But the doctor seemed kind and her hands were firm and knowledgeable. She was glad that the doctor sent the others away. A good climax or two was just what she needed. And to have Jake nearby, after all these months, reassured her that everything would be all right, no matter what the outcome of the tournament.

Irkut walked out of the first aid station with a new puzzle to decipher. Jake had told everyone that the pony who he had found was a stranger to him. He said that some people he knew in Chicago had known of her and could snatch her. He never said at anytime that he knew her. But why would the pony feel comfort at his voice if she didn't know who he was? He was sure that Jake had fucked her once or twice in the ponybarn during her training, but just that, only once or twice. Otherwise he tried to stay away from her. Irkut's instructions were that no one speak English around her during training. He had never told Jake to stay away from her. Now that he thought about it, it was odd that he didn't take a greater interest in her training since he was the one who picked her and suggested the plan to challenge Lightning to a match race. Wouldn't he have naturally been more concerned about how his plan was working out?

Irkut's suspicions just reached to a whole new level. He was sure something fishy was going on. The pony's ease at the sound of Jake's voice was just something to add to his list of unexplained circumstances, such as why the pony named Czarina had been at the Burnham mansion anyway. Who would have recruited such a behemoth and flown her in specially? And if Chocolate knew Jake before she was kidnapped, wouldn't she be enraged at the role he had played in having her reduced to little better than an animal rather than be comforted by his voice?

The suspicious driver renewed his pledge to keep a close eye on the Americans. He didn't have anything other than theories and strange circumstances as of yet. Dr. Kevsky's comment on Chocolate's reaction to Jake's voice could be seen as speculation. But like all good ponygirl doctors, she had a great deal of experience in dealing with them and knew much about their moods. Her reputation was impeccable. If he found out something more concrete, he would go straight to the Commission. Something was going on, of that he was sure.

Jake was watching the pleasant, kindly demeanored doctor apply her expert, soft hands to Chocolate's frame. She seemed to have a magic touch, for wherever her hands went, the pony began to moan and writhe on the padded table. Jake's cock was getting hard from watching the lustful pony. Tanya was right next to him and she snuck her hand over his pants and took hold of it surreptitiously, giving it a little squeeze. "So the ponygirls like you, Jake, eh? You must fuck them a lot," she said teasingly.

"No, not that much," Jake returned. Suddenly he realized the import of what Dr. Kevsky had said in front of Irkut. Jake had been wondering what Irkut had meant yesterday when he gave him that little speech about how much he cared about Kalikastan and he wouldn't let anyone harm it. This would add to whatever suspicions the man had about him. The man was no fool, that was for sure. Nor was he bedazzled by Burnham's money. He was down to earth, real, and people like that had a tendency to figure out human behavior. There was only two more days to go. Would everything hold together?

Chocolate was moaning and squirming now on the table with intensity. Her ankles tugged at the rings to which they were attached. Her nipples had grown stiff and her breath was coming hard. The lady doctor had her fingers buried in the pony's slushy crevasse. Her thumb was worrying the little nubbin of pleasure at the top. Her face looked concerned, but professional, detached. Although he suspected that she was not immune to the lustful effects of watching the large, strong, brown skinned pony in heat, she certainly wasn't letting it show.

Tanya, on the other hand was getting as randy as a rabbit. Her hip kept grinding against his and she was giving him lascivious looks. He definitely wanted to jump her bones again. He had intended to go see the slave girl he had fucked last night after Burnham's show, the cheerleader, but he might just have other plans. He wondered if he could talk Tanya into a threesome. She had had a definite interest in the Malaysian slave girl, Orchid, when she saw her in the cage in Burnham's caravan when they went there to fuck after the parade.

Chocolate seemed to be nearing her crisis. The blond doctor eased her ministrations to the pony's soft, hairless quim with her hand. She spread the pony's engorged love lips apart with her other and then leaned over and took hold of her love button with her lips. Chocolate gave out a huge moan and her body began to convulse. Her thighs shook and her hips writhed. "Mmmmmm! Mmmmmm!" she moaned through her gag. Tanya gave Jake's cock another squeeze.

Chocolate reveled in the exquisite feelings that the doctor's well trained lips were bringing her. She felt a wave of relief pass through her. Her body shook and her hips writhed. She moaned loudly as her pussy throbbed on and on.

After the pony's convulsions dwindled, and her breathing returned to normal, her body lay limp on the examining table. "She sure looks relaxed now," Tanya said playfully. "I could use some relaxation, Mr. Barnes," she added.

"Later," Jake answered her. "You heard my boss. Do you want to get me fired?"

"Yes," the impish girl replied. "Then you can come to work for Papa. He could use a man like you and so could Mama."

"I would just be afraid of what your mama would use me for," Jake threw back at her, laughing. "It would be just a little weird."

"You'd forget how weird it was when she got her mouth around your cock," Tanya said, not giving in. "I can hear Papa sometimes groaning for twenty minutes."

"That's a pleasant picture," Jake retorted. "I don't mean to be crude, but does he fuck you too?"

"Of course not, Jake" Tanya said, giving his arm a fierce slap. "What do you think we are, Romanovs or something? There has to be some standards."

"Let's let Chocolate just lie here alone and rest," Kevsky said. She had restored Chocolate's ice pack to her thigh and pulled her Velcro tabs shut over her eyes.

The trio walked to the front of the tent. "Bring Chocolate to me before the winter sets in, Mr. Barnes. I'll take her little hood off of her clit for you. It'll make her much more responsive."

"She's going to do me once the racing season is over," Tanya said. "Then I'll be like a tiger!" She emphasized her prediction by making her hand into a little claw and scrunching up her face.

"Well, technically, she's not mine," Jake answered.

"Oh, she's your all right," the doctor replied. "You just don't own her. I have a sixth sense when it comes to ponygirls and slave girls. I felt the connection between you two right away."

Jake really wanted to change the subject. "Well, I'll talk to Mr. Burnham about it," he said.

"Come and visit my lab," the pretty doctor said. "I'm experimenting with some behavioral techniques that I think will be helpful in slave girl training. It's harsh, but I've had some very good results. If I had a little bit more funding…." The doctor smiled and shrugged her shoulders. "But isn't that what all mad scientists say?"

It was hard for Jake to envision the beautiful doctor with such sensitive hands inflicting cruelties on piteously frightened, newly kidnapped, young women. It was like there was some drug in the air here that made people yearn to cause suffering. He had caught it, he knew that. He had felt his pulse racing when he brought the whip to bear on his slave girl, Dana. He had to hold himself in check lest he do her some real damage. It was definitely time to go. Who knows what he would become if he stayed?

"Let's go see my mother's race," Tanya suggested. "She's running very soon."

"Go ahead," Dr. Kevsky interjected. "I'll hold the fort. There's another hour and a half before Chocolate's race. I'll give her some more relief in a little while."

"A case in point," Jake thought. He would enjoy seeing the naked Irish women, or former women, as the case may be, throw their whole beings into entertaining a crowd of people inured to their suffering. It was going to delight him to see them groaning and straining to produce their best for their cruel mistress, their big breasts bobbing, their naked sexes dripping with sweat. And tonight, he would probably fuck one of them. And it didn't bother him one bit.

From the first aid tent they were able to get a position right on the rail. They heard the race being announced. Jake and Tanya's position was outside of the grandstand area, right next to the final turn before the home stretch. It would be a great place to watch from, closer than Jake had ever been to one of the big races.

The cabriolet, like the landau, was a 3000 meter race. It took a lot of stamina for the naked, former women to haul the carriage twice around the track. The broughams and the troikas ran a 1500 meter course as did the yearlings. There, speed was the prime factor. In the longer races it was endurance.

Jake still had the binoculars from earlier in the day. Helena came trotting past where they stood, having warmed her ponies up with a quick turn around the track.

She gave the lovers a little wink as she passed them and headed up to the start line. Helena's opponents wore black and silver hoods. They had uniformly black ponytails and were as pale as snow. The crowd silenced itself down to a murmur as it awaited the start gun. When it went off, the crowd came back to life, all the punters screaming for their favorites.

Twelve frantic ponies dug their boots into the dirt for all they were worth and took off down the track. The other team was a higher seed and so was assigned the outside track, a break for Helena. Jake watched through the glasses as the two teams approached the quarter turn and veered towards their left.

"Let me see! Let me see!" Tanya exclaimed, jumping up and down next to him. Jake handed her the glasses. The ponies were at the half pole on the long, back straightaway. In a few moments they would come roaring by.

3000 meters is a little over 1 ¾ miles. A fast human being can do a mile in six minutes, a very fast one five. Six, highly trained, human-like females, driven by a deeply ingrained fear of the whip, hauling a 350 pound carriage and a 150 pound driver can make a mile in about eight minutes. So one lap around the track was about seven. Mathematically, this meant that the coaches covered about 645 feet in a minute, or almost 10 feet every second. It's not what you would call zooming, but when the feat was being accomplished by six deliciously formed, naked females, pulling frantically in their harnesses, their chests near to burst, straining with the arduousness of their task, it was something to see. Especially up close.

Jake had never heard a large pony team really strug-gling to achieve top speed over a long course. In their training sessions, their drivers usually concentrated on several kilometers long endurance runs with short bursts of speed in between. Running a large ponygirl team at full tilt hauling a heavy load was a prescription for injury. A large team depended greatly on the coordination of the ponies and so an individual pony which suffered an injury was not easily replaced. While he had seen them run along the practice track back at Burnham's estate while standing at the rail, he had never seen them in action like this up close.

When the two teams entered the turn from the straightaway, Helena's was slightly ahead. No more than thirty feet separated Jake from the two sets of highly charged ponies. They issued high pitched, feminine grunts and groans as they ran, their voices muted not entirely by the cruel bits in their mouths. Breasts flew this way and that. Dirt kicked up as their boots dug deeply into the track. Their bodies were slick with sweat, shiny, as if they had been covered with a coat of varnish. Long, thick black and orange ponytails fluttered behind them, jerking back and forth as they recorded the ponies' shift from one foot to the other. Their shoulders shifted back and forth, their useless hands fastened behind them

They went by in what seemed like a flash. Helena and the other driver were yelling and cursing at their charges, urging them to employ every ounce of their strength. It was marvelous to watch the drivers guide the ponies through the turn. Even though the ponies' eye flaps were up, enabling them to see the track in front of them, their training was so thorough that they would have crashed right into the rail if their drivers had not signaled them properly through their reins.

As the two teams finished the turn and entered the home straightaway, Jake was overwhelmed by what he had just witnessed. "Wow," he just said.

"Do you understand?" Tanya asked him.

Yes, he understood. He recalled Irkut's statement yesterday about how Kalikastan was a special place with special institutions. He was damn right!

Jake took back the binoculars and watched the teams dash off for another lap of the track. The lead had changed hands and the black tailed team was now slightly ahead. His stomach fluttered with anxiety as he watched it gain ground against Helena's. Its driver was making his move early, perhaps trying to strain the endurance of the lower seed team.

The gap between the teams widened as they coursed over the back stretch. Tanya had taken the glasses and was screaming, "Come on, Mama! Come on, Mama!" over and over again. As the two teams entered the turn just before the ¾ mark, Helena made her move. Jake saw her give a dramatic snap of the reins. Her carriage seemed to accelerate immediately. As they came by where Jake and Tanya stood, the orange tailed team was rapidly gaining ground.

If the ponies were strained at their task on the first lap, their efforts seemed heroic on the second. Red colored their chests above their breasts. The grunting and groaning had increased, mixed with animalistic snorts as they took in air through their mouths and noses. Their hooded, faceless heads were bent determinedly to their task. Helena and the other driver had their whips out, ready to bring them into action once they had negotiated the turn. There was an intense, almost fiendish grimace on the gray haired woman's face. It was easy to see the great excitement she experienced in driving her naked, female chargers to the utmost of their endurance.

Helena was still gaining as the carriages passed through the turn, although the black tailed team's speed had picked up too. Watching the teams go down the track through the home stretch, it was impossible to see from their vantage point which team had the lead. Had Helena peaked too late? Would her ponies hold up for the 400 hundred or so meters to the finish line? It was the only time Jake wished he was up in his seat in the grandstands so he could see the teams cross it.

As they passed over the line that demarked the end of the race, an official on the sideline flicked a checkered flag. Tanya and Jake's eyes went immediately to the tote board atop the fence on the outside of the far stretch. For several long seconds the tension was almost unbearable. And then the light went on next to the symbol for the red, blue and green team. Tanya screeched her joy and bounced up and down. Jake felt a thrill for the older lady. She had survived to the second day.

Tanya insisted they proceed immediately to the winner's circle. Helena and the other driver were taking their teams through a cool down lap. When they crossed in front of the grandstand, Helena stood at her perch atop the carriage and waved her hat at the crowd. There were cheers and an undercurrent of boos. It seemed some fans were not quite so equinanimous as Irkut was about the fact of a woman driver.

Jake and Tanya were waiting in the winner's circle when Helena pulled her team into it. The father, Vassily, had come down from the owner's booth together with his sons. Helena jumped down from the driver's seat and gave him a big hug. No matter what happened tomorrow, today had been a success. In their first ever tournament, they had made it to the later rounds. One loss tomorrow and they would be out, but for tonight, they could savor their accomplishment.

The ponies were still huffing and puffing from their ordeal. No smiles had broken out among the faceless ponies, none jumped for joy or celebrated their achievement. Perhaps they experienced some relief that tonight they would not be beaten. But if they did, you could not tell. They were as silent and seemingly indifferent to their victory as they would have been if they were real ponies. Their strong, muscular bodies glowed from their efforts. Their breasts swayed and flowed as their chests went up and down. Sweat ran down their shoulders and was literally dripping off of their nipples onto the dirt track. There were red marks where the harnesses had dug deep into their skin. Tomorrow, they would do it all over again.

Tanya's lithesome sisters were there too. They had ponygirl water jugs in their hands and they were giving each pony a mouthful. You didn't want to water them too much after a race or they would experience cramps, but it was important that the ponies' needs be seen to right away. It seemed only fair given the wonderful display they had just given. When done, the girls too hugged their mother.

A racing official came over and gave Helena a small medal marking her accomplishment of winning the heat. If she did not win another, this small, gold medallion would serve as the emblem of her ponies' feat. Copies could be made to dangle from their collars as a reward for all their hard work. It would set them off from the other ponies who had not yet garnered any glory, even if minor.

When the family's celebrations waned, Jake raised his pinioned wrist to Vassily. "I've got to get this thing off of me," he said. "We've got some serious problems and I need to be available for my boss."

"Sure, sure," Vassily said. Tanya pouted while he unlocked the handcuffs.

"You had better come by the campsite later," she said petulantly. "If you don't, I'll never marry you."

"Ha, ha!" erupted her father. "Don't ever give a bachelor a way out, my dear. Say that you'll never forgive him, but don't let him off the hook!"

"All right then," she said, rubbing her body against Jake's lasciviously. "I won't ever forgive you until the next time you fuck me."

Jake smiled. "I'll try. It all depends on my boss. If not, I'll see you in the morning."

Tanya threw her arms around his shoulders and gave him a hearty, lustful kiss. "Good luck with Chocolate. Make sure she gets a good fucking tonight. She deserves it."

A half hour later, Jake was watching Giorgi hook the wounded ponygirl back up to her cart outside the first aid station. She was clearly in pain every time she put her left leg down. She would walk through this race but they wouldn't know if she had to race again until after dinner time.

With a double elimination tournament, it was important that some teams get sent home early on so that the racing does not go on forever. As a pony with one loss, the race that was coming up, Chocolate would be prime to be chosen to run one more. It would be based on which pony had been lost to. Since the pony Chocolate was 'running' now had a high seed, Chocolate's upcoming defeat by it made her a prime candidate for being chosen to run again.

The crowd cheered and applauded when Chocolate was brought up to the line. Based on Chocolate's injury and the fact that there was virtually no chance for her to win the race unless the other pony dropped dead on the track or somehow defaulted, the masters of the tournament had suspended betting for this race.

The gun went off and Chocolate began a slow lope down the track, managed carefully by her dwarfish driver. The other pony got off to a good start, but once it had gotten about ten lengths ahead, it began to cruise.

It took Chocolate about ten minutes to complete the circuit. The memories of crowds are fickle and by the time she reached the finish line, limping noticeably along, its interest had gone on to the next race.

Giorgi took Chocolate back to the first aid tent where Dr. Kevsky was waiting for her. She was placed back up on the examining table and her bit was removed, only to be replaced by her leather gag. The doctor gave her leg another rubdown and then placed the ice pack back on it. All they could do now was wait.

They wouldn't know for at least an hour and a half so Giorgi went back to his encampment. He had a slave girl there who had just spent the last two hours bound and gagged, kneeling in the dirt. He would free her and send her for his dinner. When he was done, he intended to return to the first aid station to await the verdict of chance.

Irkut was waiting at the aid station when they arrived. He watched the doctor minister to the pony for a few minutes and then said that he was going to report to Mr. Burnham on the pony's condition. He would also go by the tournament masters' booth to make sure there was no funny business regarding the race selection.

Jake had nothing to do but wait. All his work of the last ten months would come down to whether Chocolate had to run another race today. He stepped out of the tent and lit a Lucky Strike, pondering the vagaries of fate.

CHAPTER FOUR

Up in the owner's booth, Drabik was beside himself with joy. It seemed that his plan had worked. Watching Chocolate hobble around the track, he doubted very much that she would be able to race tomorrow. And there was still the chance that she could be eliminated tonight.

A large breasted, blond haired slave girl passed by him carrying a tray of food. Her slave name, tattooed across her upper chest, above her breasts, was Thea. She wore the tattoo of a fierce mountain lion on her lower belly, denoting the House where she had received her initial slave training. Drabik snaked out his hand and captured her arm.

"Where are you going, slave girl?" he asked her.

"I, I, I have to take this tray down to the buffet, master," she said nervously. All the slave girls had noticed the dark, brooding man sitting in the booth all afternoon. Word had spread among them about who he was and to avoid him at all costs. The blond girl was hoping that he would let her go on about her business.

"Hey, you," Drabik called out to another slave girl, a thin brunette with long, straight hair. "Where are you going?" he asked her.

"To pick up some dirty dishes and bring them downstairs to the kitchen, master," she said tremulously. The blond girl's hopes rose that she would be spared an interlude with the man the other girls had said was a notorious killer and abuser of slave girls. She didn't have anything against the brunette. She didn't even know her. It was just that if she had to choose between herself and the other girl it would be the other girl every time.

"Take this tray down to the buffet," Drabik commanded the brunette. A wave of relief passed over her face.

The blond girl's heart sank. Drabik still had a fierce grip on her arm and his fingers were digging deeply into her flesh. He pulled the frightened girl to the front of him as the brunette scurried away.

The girl had a round, innocent face, a face that belonged on a soap commercial, not on a voluptuous slave girl. Her hips were wide. Her areolas were dark and spread over the tips of her beauteous breasts with a diameter of almost three inches. They were truly a marvel. In the centers were two, fat, juicy looking nipples.

Thea was Lithuanian. Although her native land was a former Soviet Republic, the ban on poaching for slave girls in Russia and the Ukraine did not apply to it. The Lithuanian nation was more Germanic than Slavs. And they too once had an empire which had encompassed the nomadic tribes of Kalikastan. So their females were fair game.

She had been a slave for a little over three years. Her current master was her fifth. She had served in a whorehouse in Dlitski, in a nightclub as special 'entertainment' and on three estates. Everyone seemed fascinated by her tits. When she had been free, she had been proud of their heavy, firm bulk and the sensuousness of her outstandingly large areolas. She had had a few lovers while attending the university in Vilnius and when their mouths subsumed the smooth, dark sea that surrounded her nipples, she would almost faint.

Now, however, she cursed the fate that made her breasts so appealing. It was one of her former boyfriends who had sold her into slavery. She had dumped him because of his drug addiction. One day, he had called her and asked her to meet him somewhere, that it was urgent that he speak to her. He was crying on the telephone and she felt sorry for him. When she arrived at the remote cottage where he said he was staying, she had been unceremoniously stripped and bound by the men that she found there. When they pulled off her blouse and bra, they marveled at what was revealed. Bound, gagged and blindfolded, in her terror, she overheard one of them say that her old boyfriend had told them the truth about her tits.

At the slave training center, her breasts were savagely misused. Her stint at the whorehouse hadn't been too bad. The owner had selected her for her marvelous mammaries and made sure that they were not the subject of too much abuse, since they were a major draw. In the nightclub, her act consisted mainly of letting several customers a night fuck her between her pretty globes while she sucked at the head of their cocks each time they emerged from the tunnel formed by her conjoined mounds. Her life on the estates had been hard. She was frequently whipped on her breasts by her owners and was almost always the whore of choice for any guests. Her new owner, she had only been with him for several weeks, seemed a cut above the rest, but he too amused himself often by pinching and pulling painfully on her breasts' unusually decorous tips.

Drabik eyed the fantastic pair of fleshy mounds lustfully. He grabbed her nipples between the forefingers and thumbs of his hands and squeezed them tightly, increasing the pressure gradually, until the girl moaned with discomfort and then pain. Each of the racing ponygirl owners had contributed one or two slave girls to the kitchens for the duration of the tournament. There were several of Grobgy's sluts running around the place. It was understood that they would be available for use during the night when the racing came to a halt. Drabik decided that Thea would be his companion for the evening. But first he wanted her to suck his cock.

"Get on your knees, whore and put your lips around my prick," he told her coarsely. "If you make me come before I'm ready, you'll wish you had died yesterday."

Trembling, the naked, big breasted girl fell to her knees before the cruel killer. She believed him when he promised fierce retribution for displeasing him. Once again, she had her breasts to blame for her misfortunes.

Thea's straw blond hair was thick but cut short, just below the level of her ears, exposing her soft, pale neck. Nervously, she opened Drabik's pants and drew his thickening wand from them. She pursed her lips, centered them on the stiff pole and took possession of the long, thick, hard rod with her mouth.

Drabik moaned with pleasure as the experienced mouth drove his lust. The girl had an active, nimble tongue and he sighed as she washed the shaft of his cock with it. Her hands were behind her back and she used only her mouth to pleasure him. Her voluminous breasts rubbed against his thighs pleasantly.

Leaning his head back, Drabik congratulated himself on the success of his scheme to put Chocolate out of the tournament. He had told the stupid driver to meet his men right after the race when they were to give him his money and help him flee. Drabik had promised him a small fortune and, since his driving career was already on the skids, he had accepted with visions of retiring to a villa on the Black Sea or maybe a small Greek island. The men Drabik had chosen to take the driver for a ride were handpicked members of his conspiracy against Grobgy, his future lieutenants. Right now, the driver was sucking mud deep in the neighboring forest, a bullet in the back of his head. No one would ever connect Drabik to the foul that Chocolate had suffered.

The slave girl brought all the skills developed over three years as an abject whore to her pleasuring of the frightful man's cock. She prayed that he would be satisfied with her oral attentions and find some other poor wench to spend the evening with. Her stomach roiled with fear as her lips stroked the shaft of his rigid pole. She teased the underside of his glans with her tongue and sucked gently on the fatty helmet atop it. Thea poised herself to glean every nuance of the man's excitement lest she send him over the top too soon. When she pressed her face down onto his belly, taking his length into her throat, his thighs began to quake and she feared that she had gone too far. She pulled her head back quickly and paused her efforts, just keeping the tip of her tongue tantalizing the tiny opening at the cock's tip

Drabik was enjoying the slut's efforts. Any blowjob would have been a good one with the way he felt, but he had to admit that the girl was exceptionally skilled. He felt his crisis approaching and waited to see if the girl would give him the excuse he looked for to deliver a torrent of agonizing blows to her body. When she pulled back and saved herself, he felt a little disappointed, as if some opportunity had been missed. Of course, he needed no excuse to beat the slave. Her owner wouldn't object unless he permanently damaged her. Even then, an exchange of cash or the delivery of a suitable substitute slut would assuage his pique.

Finally, as naked ponygirls plied the oval dirt track below the owner's booth window, his lusts grew too large to contain.

"Now!" he ordered the frightened girl. She accelerated her motions on his cock. Her head bobbed up and down and her tongue worked frantically to excite him. When his cock commenced its gyrations in her mouth, she pushed herself down until she could feel the pulsing of the thick meat in her throat and his thick spewm being jetted down it.

The killer groaned with pleasure. Some of the other jaded men in the booth looked over and laughed. They knew what Drabik was experiencing. It was a joy to spill oneself into the mouth of a subservient slut, to know that she had no power to refuse it.

Drabik sighed deeply as his cock came to rest. He ran his hand through the hair of the whore between his knees. Maybe he would take her to his tent and play some games with her, her thought. Lightning had run and won all of her races. The selection for the evening races would not be posted for another hour or so. He had time to kill, and the slut had two wonderful breasts that begged the attention of a whip.

"Close me up," Drabik ordered the big breasted girl. Her hands shaking, she tucked away his fleshy weapon and carefully pulled his zipper up, securing the softened pole in its lodgment. She was too afraid to stand without the man's permission. Kneeling there, her fate in the balance, she felt the urge to cry.

Rising from his seat, Drabik ordered the girl to follow him. Near the door to the public portion of the grandstand, there was a cabinet which contained many of the accouterments used and useful in the abuse of slave girls. Drabik stopped there and retrieved a thick, leather gag. He turned to the girl. "Open your mouth," he said coldly.

Thea was beside herself. The man would not be gagging her if he did not mean to take her away. Her knees felt weak and her eyes grew watery. She obeyed nonetheless and quickly had her oral cavern filled with dank tasting leather.

"Turn around," Drabik ordered her. When she was facing away from him, he joined her hands together behind her by her slave bracelets. He let her stand there, miserable and frightened as he rooted around in the cabinet for something special. When his search proved fruitful, he ordered the girl to turn once more and face him.

He had retrieved two, large, powerful clamps from the cabinet. He took hold of one of the girl's fat nipples and pulled it out from her body. The girl gave a moan as she watched the serrated jaws of the large, cruel implement approach her tender teat. When the man closed them over her flesh, the teeth biting deeply into her areola, she groaned with pain. Her knees were shaking and her belly all aflutter with fear. The cruel man locked another clamp on her opposite breast. The bite of the clamp felt like a dozen tiny knives piercing her skin.

Drabik looked into the terrified girl's face and smiled. He was going to enjoy this one. Tears had brimmed in her eyes and sweat had formed on her graceful forehead. Her innocent face was counterpunctual to her erotically charged body. Her hips were wide and her belly flat. She had long, solid thighs, well sculpted and made for the riding crop. And her breasts, they were twin gifts of nature. Although the mammaries were large, they were not grotesque or out of place on the girl's slightly heavy frame. She was built to wear them.

Anxious to get the frightened female alone in his tent, Drabik took a small chain and hooked the two tortured tits together. He hooked a five foot long leash to the middle of it. "Come along, little slave girl," he told her. "We have a date."

He led the whining female from the owners' booth by her leash. He kept up a brisk pace as he passed through the crowded hallways of the grandstand. People stopped and stared jealously at his voluptuous prisoner. A naked women was being led bound and gagged past a crowd of seemingly normal, everyday people and not one of them thought the sight unusual or out of place. Naked slave girls were scurrying all around the public portion of the building, carrying trays of food for their masters, running bets or just trying to find places to hide. Drabik was not the only one with a beautiful, naked woman in tow.

People just tended to get out of the way when Drabik walked along a public place. His demeanor bespoke a hard, remorseless man quick to anger or to take offense. The crowd parted as he hauled the young girl along.

Thea was moaning and crying as she stumbled after the man who had captured her. Her nipples were sending her intense jolts of pain. Not satisfied to have her merely walking behind him, every once in a while the cruel man gave a tug on the leash as if to hurry her along, but really just to add to her anguish.

The couple left the clubhouse and trekked along the well worn pathway to the restricted camping area. The people passing in the other direction, many of them acquaintances of the killer, smiled and nodded to him, knowingly.

When they reached Drabik's tent, he removed the leash from the chains that connected her bruised and battered nipples. Tears were flowing down the pretty girl's face. He left her standing there for a moment as he retrieved a longer chain from a trunk. He brought it over to her and connected one end to the chain linking her breasts. He tossed the other end over a pole that went horizontally across the top of the tent. The free end of the chain came down to within a few inches of the unhappy girl's ankles. Drabik went back to his trunk and returned with a one pound weight. He lifted the end of the chain and attached the weight to it. Then, holding it in his hand, he smiled at her and let it drop.

Thea panicked when she saw the man release the weight. It fell several feet and then jerked back. She gave out a scream of anguish as the chain transferred the energy from the falling weight to her nipples. "Aaaaaaaauuugh!" she cried out from behind her gag. She rose on her tippy toes to try and assuage the tension on the chain. If she rose high enough, the bottom of the weight just barely touched the floor of the tent, easing somewhat the pressure on her sore teats. After a few moments, however, her toes and the arches of her feet began to ache. She knew that she could not maintain the posture for long.

"I'm going to get my dinner," Drabik told her. "I'll leave you here to play with the weight until I come back." He gave a little laugh.

The girl's eyes went wide with horror. She tried to plead with the evil man, but her voice was muffled and distorted. She gave a moan of despair as Drabik turned and left the tent.

Several of the estates were hosting buffets and Drabik went and sought out one of them. He did not want to see

Anya and so he walked some distance away from his own tent. He found a party going on sponsored by an estate whose owners he knew well and he joined them.

A lamb was roasting over a spit and there was a large pot filled with roasted peppers, mushrooms, onions and potatoes. He grabbed a plateful of food and sat down with one of the trainers from the other estate. There was a pitcher of ale on the table and he poured himself a flagon full of it.

"Next tournament, it'll be me throwing the party," he thought as he tore into his food. "I'll be the big shot the people will bow and scrape to. And Lightning will be mine. I'll harness her to a cart and have her take me everywhere. And then I'll fuck her until my balls turn blue."

As he was eating, the runners in the final 1500 meter sulky race were being announced. He stilled himself so that he would not miss it. Sure enough, his luck was holding. Chocolate was named as one of the contesting ponies. The other was Vixen, the one from the south which was second seed. It was all over but the weeping. The race was in about twenty minutes. He decided that his date with the big breasted blond girl could wait. She certainly wasn't going anywhere. He finished off his double pint sized stein of ale and got up to walk over to the grandstands.

* * * * * * * * * * * * * *

Jake, Irkut and Giorgi stood outside the first aid tent solemnly taking in the news. Someone had produced a bottle of vodka and they all took a long pull on it before anyone spoke.

"Well, that's that," Jake said. "All our work was for nothing."

"Not to mention the pony's work too," Irkut said. "She deserved a chance at a championship. She has great spirit. Maybe in the spring…."

Giorgi sat down in the dirt. Tears were coming to his eyes. Jerzi would best him again this year. It would have been beautiful, showing up in the brand new fancy, sulky cart to his brother's amazement, having his pony run the other one into the ground. He was certain that Chocolate could have beaten her.

"Well, what do we do now?" Jake asked. "I don't want to talk to Burnham about it. He'll be madder than a wet hen."

Actually, the billionaire was not that upset at all. It only meant that he would not get a chance to acquire Lightning. He would have loved to have the two fastest ponies in the country. A double gold medal in the 1500 and the 3000 next spring would have been immensely satisfying. He did, though, still have one of the fastest ponies, Chocolate. No way was he going to let Jake take her out of the country. He could renew his challenge against Lightning next year. It meant that Maddy would have to spend the winter and the spring as a ponygirl, but he hadn't intended to free her anyway.

When she had been his sparkly, somewhat naïve, young, only niece, he had felt great affection for her. She was the sole beneficiary in his will. But Maddy didn't exist anymore. She was only Lightning. He had watched her run today, shutting down her opposition. She was a lovely sight with more than ample breasts and a gracious form. She was even trimmer than he remembered her. He wouldn't mind fucking her himself. In fact he had planned to do it in celebration if they had been able to pull off the match race and win it.

He was sitting in the owner's booth, a nubile slave girl folded over his lap. His hand was in her quim and he was stroking her to orgasm absent mindedly. She had mid-length, black hair and was thin with moderate, round breasts. He hadn't decided whether to take her back to his caravan tonight. He still had the Malaysian slut there and she was proving to be a delight. She cowered and cried as he abused her with the whip and she moaned unhappily when he pierced her body with his prick. He doubted that he would get the same pleasure from fucking the undeniably delightful cunt draped over his lap. But, he thought, maybe he didn't want to work tonight. He could let the black haired girl do all the work and just lie back and enjoy it. He would contemplate the irony that Maddy's kidnapping had brought him to this paradise while the black haired girl rode his prick. And, come to think of it, since Maddy was now a ponygirl and it looked like she could very well remain one permanently, he had to think about changing his Will.

* * * * * * * * * * * * * * *

Down at the first aid tent, the three men were still moping about the vagaries of fate. Chocolate lay inside the tent peacefully. It was about ten minutes before post time. Once Chocolate failed to show, the other pony would do a victory lap and be declared the winner.

Svetlana Kevsky came out of the tent. "It's too bad," she said. "I hate to think of her just forfeiting like that. I can tell she has a lot of fight."

Giorgi's head perked up. "You're right," he said. "Why should she go out meekly? Let's hook her up and at least start the race. She can finish walking, but she'll finish with honor."

The other men agreed. Irkut and Jake ran into the tent and unhooked the pony from her table. They eased her damaged leg to the floor and helped her hobble out. Giorgi had her harness and cart all ready for her.

Irkut began to strap the pony into its harness while Jake stood in front of her. He was remembering the whore he had saved and used to fuck back in Chicago. It was hard to conceive of her and this creature as the same being. She was so brazenly nude and faceless now. Her body was hard and sculpted. He reached down and caressed her hairless slit while Irkut tightened the straps on her body. "Too bad, Chocolate," he thought. "It's a sad way to end."

Irkut expertly guided Chocolate in between the twin poles that led from the sulky and attached them to her hips. He fastened the straps that led to her waist behind her back and to her shoulders, making sure that they had the proper tension. When he was done, he stepped back to appreciate the sight of the pony ready to do battle. He wasn't sure what was up with Jake and the former female. All he knew was that she deserved another chance to come back with the gold in the spring. She could go head to head against Lightning in the 3000 or wipe up the 1500 meter class now that she wouldn't have to try and train for both races.

Giorgi settled into his seat and gave the other men a nod. He gave the reins a little jerk and the pony obediently began to trot unsteadily to the starting post.

Chocolate knew that something bad had happened. She could just tell it from the demeanor of the men. Her leg still hurt terribly, although the kindly doctor had relaxed her muscles by bringing her to several thrilling orgasms over the last several hours. Her mission was over. She knew that. It was hard to accept, but as she followed her driver's directions to the gate that led onto the track, she was not sad that this would be her last performance as a ponygirl. She wanted to be Jackie again, see the sights of home, put her own hands on her pussy from time to time or even scratch her nose. And she wanted to decide who she would fuck. Jake was on the top of her list. She would give him an evening that he would never forget when they got back to the States.

Chocolate's opponent, sporting a red and black hood, was waiting for her at the start line. Vixen was an Alsatian pony, two years to her bit. She was fast and just coming into her own as the season had come to an end. It was the perfect time for her to blossom.

The black haired, naked, former human female, with four, full racing seasons under her belt, knew what she was about. Her reactions to her driver's flick of the reins were almost extra sensory. Her thighs were thick and muscular. She was colored a pale white. Her breasts were round and high on her chest. Her kidnapping was virtually an accident. She had been home on a visit from the technical college in Rheims and had decided to go out for a walk on a sunny, cloudless day. She had just turned nineteen and, as nineteen year olds often are, was in love with a boy back at school. He had asked her to marry him and she had taken the time off to be at home with her family, away from him, to consider it. They were both young and there was so much she wanted to do. But they were in love and love must have its way.

The men were on their way to an isolated farmhouse where several girls who had been harvested from various urban areas of France were being kept before being taken out to a makeshift airfield where a plane was to come in and then fly them to Kalikastan. The men saw the broad shouldered, but shapely girl walking down the narrow country lane. She had a sprig of heather in her hands. She smiled at them when they slowed and then stopped the van next to her. She had just opened her mouth to see if they were lost when the sliding door to the van sprung open. Strong, male hands grabbed her by the front of her blouse and dragged her in. The van door slid shut and the van took off, leaving the sprig of heather that the startled girl had been holding lying in the middle of the road. Three hours later, she was sobbing, naked, bound and gagged and huddled in a tiny cage in the cargo compartment of a large, propeller driven aircraft heading east.

Giorgi knew the other driver well. They had been pals and drinking buddies for many years. He was a dwarf, like Giorgi, and hailed from Kazakhstan. His Muslim background didn't prevent him from downing shot after shot of vodka while watching a lithesome slave girl do her thing on a stage in a nightclub in Dlitski. The short people hung together. When the race was over, Giorgi decided that he would go over to Hakim's campsite and get roaring drunk.

Everyone knew what was happening. This was Chocolate's swan song in the tournament. The sun had long ago faded and the track was brightly lit by overhead lights. From the track, you could barely see into the grandstands. The crowd was giving desultory cheers and some people were applauding politely Chocolate's gesture of showing up for the race at all. The sounds emerged eerily from amidst the darkness caused by the glare of the overhead lights.

The bright bulbs made the colors of the drivers' uniforms seem almost garish. The pale skin of Vixen seemed pasty while Chocolate's darker hue almost seemed pale. The two ponies posed themselves in their starting positions. Vixen knew nothing about the problems the other pony was facing and was prepared to let all her energy out in a single minded rush to victory. Chocolate did not know that, had she not been injured, the other pony was her only true competitor in the tournament. But what the ponies didn't know, everyone else did. There were some sighs of disappointment from the fans, sad that the storybook ending to Chocolate's marvelous season had not come true. Others rued the fact that the much looked forward to contest between the two wonderful ponies had been reduced to this.

The race official yelled "Ready!" and raised his arm in the air. He paused for three seconds and then pulled the trigger of the starting gun. At the sound of the blank cartridge going off, the two ponies jumped into action.

Vixen pulled away from the injured pony immediately. Chocolate, bitter that her driver allowed the other pony to show her up so, began her long, sad trot around the track. By the time that Chocolate reached the half way pole, the black tailed pony was approaching the finish line. Giorgi just gave the reins a little tweak and increased Chocolate's speed marginally.

It was when he heard the growing commotion from the crowd that Giorgi knew that something was up. It grew from a murmur, to an excited roar. He looked up at the tote board and saw that Vixen had not yet crossed the finish line. It was impossible for her not have done so. They were almost nine minutes into the race.

It was when he came out of the turn just before the home straightaway that he saw what had happened. Vixen was standing still, her driver calmly perched upon the seat of her sulky cart, just yards from the chalk mark that marked the race's end. Vixen had won all of her races that day. She could afford one loss. Other than Chocolate, there was no other 1500 pony in the same class as her. As a gesture to his fellow driver and in a respectful nod towards the abilities of the famously heroic Chocolate, Hakim was going to let Chocolate win. The pony would survive for another day! Maybe, just maybe, her leg would heal enough for her to finish off her other competitors and be ready to meet Vixen in the championship race some 40 hours or so away.

Jake and Irkut had taken seats in the stands. Jake had ordered a double gin on ice from a slave girl and was downing it in what he predicted would be a night to outshine all other nights. All his dastardly deeds had gone for naught. He was unused to defeat. There was one thing he knew for sure, though. He would get Jackie out or die trying.

The noise of the crowd grew slowly. The thoughts of the fans were mostly on the next race. They were going over programs and debating the merits of the two contestants. When the lights did not flash as a victorious pony crossed the finish line, people began to turn their heads. There was Vixen, standing as still as if she were a statue. The driver was picking at his fingernails while the pony's owner strode up and down the rail cursing and swearing at him.

Irkut saw it before Jake did. He gave a huge hoot and slapped Jake on the back, spilling most of his gin. Jake looked up. The sight of the statuesque pony was incongruous and for a moment the import of what he was seeing didn't register. Then it hit him. He gave a shout and began slapping Irkut back. The two men grabbed each other's shoulders and leapt up and down for joy.

Giorgi had to wipe his eyes with his sleeves to keep the tears from falling down his cheeks. He flicked the reins to get Chocolate to go a little faster. The pony wondered what the need was, but obeyed unquestioningly. And then she saw it. She couldn't believe it. Were these people crazy? Was this sport so important to them that the other driver would even consider throwing the race so she could stay in the tournament? Pride rose up in her naked breasts. Her movements became a little more sharp. Her vision through the tiny holes in her face encompassing hood became blurry as tears filled her eyes. "What am I crying for," she said to herself. "Am I as crazy as they are?"

Suddenly, she realized what being a ponygirl meant. She was an iconic creature for whom the petty problems of these people's lives could be put away. She had sacrificed dearly so that these people could bask in her accomplishments. All that had been done to her had been necessary in order to make possible this noble gesture. She was mad; she knew it, because for that few moments, as she approached the finish line, she reveled in what she had become.

The crowd had gone wild. Programs were thrown in the air and people, strangers, were hugging and kissing one another. Was there anywhere a sport like ponygirl racing in Kalikastan? Anyone in the crowd that night would have answered a loud, emphatic "No!"

When her driver signaled her to begin her cantering steps, Chocolate raised her knees high and sprung forwards as if she had never been injured. It was her return of the crowd's salute. Giorgi doffed his cap and, after saluting Hakim, his friend, turned and waved it at the crowd. He let the pony cantor for a few more feet as the checkered flag came down and then snapped the reins. He was taking his pony home.

* * * * * * * * * * * * * *

In the opposite side of the grandstands from Jake and Irkut, Drabik was having an apoplectic fit. What did he have to do to have this weight taken from around his neck? First Lightning was injured and, for a while, it seemed the answer to his problem. But noooooo! Lightning was apparently all fixed up and well poised to win a gold medal. Now Chocolate had escaped a trap that he had taken so much trouble to devise and had murdered a man for! What was it going to take? It seemed as if the ponies were destined to meet in the match race and that was that! He had a huge ball of rage aflame in his belly and he knew how he was going to alleviate it.

The tall, well built killer exited the grandstands striding blindly through the crowd. He took no notice of anyone on the trek back to his tent. When he stepped inside, he saw the moaning and crying form of the blond haired slave girl. She was bobbing on her toes, unable to keep herself mounted on them for more than a few seconds due to the pain in her feet. Each time she lowered herself, her breasts sent her an agonizing stream of pain. Her face was wet from her tears and her body was shaking. She flinched when she saw her tormentor come back into the tent, sure that his reappearance could only bring her more agony.

Thea could see that something had animated the man into a terrible rage. Before he was just coldly cruel. Now, she anticipated receiving the full brunt of his anger. "Oh, god! Oh, god!" she exclaimed to herself. She wished that there was somewhere that she could run and hide, but there was to be no escaping her cruel fate.

Drabik stepped up to the girl and released the clamp on her right breast. The girl howled in pain as the blood returned to her injured teat. He waited until she had absorbed its full impact before releasing the other tit. She howled again, but this time, released from the chain that had held her in place, she collapsed to her knees on the floor of the tent.

Dolefully, she looked up at the angered man. "...eeeeease!" she begged loudly through her gag. "...eeeeease ont urt eeeee! ...eeease!"

Drabik was in no mood to consider the caterwauling of a slave girl. He grabbed her by the hair and pulled her to her feet. She screamed at the pain to her scalp. He spun her around and released her bound wrists from behind her back. Frantic, and against all of her training, the girl tried to flee. She got one step away when Drabik grabbed her arm and pulled her back. In a trice he had joined her hands together in front of her and connected them to the end of the chain that led up to the bar across the ceiling of his tent. When he released her, she tried to run off again, but he had taken hold of the other end of the chain and merely pulled on it until her joined hands were jerked back and they began to ride over her head. When the struggling, writhing, pretty, young slave girl was hoisted up, her toes dragging across the floor of the tent, he affixed the free end of the chain off to a hook on one of the tent poles.

Dangling in front of the cruel man, sobbing, Thea kicked her feet out futilely. Her damaged breasts swayed and jumped as she writhed helplessly. Drabik retrieved the two vicious clamps and knelt in front of the unhappy slave girl. He pushed her weak legs apart and opened one of the clamps. With his other hand, he joined together her hairless love lips and closed the sharp toothed instrument on them. The girl gave a howl of pain and her legs jerked and spasmed. Drabik had joined the delicate lips at the top of her sexual divide. He took the other clamp and affixed it to the tender flesh at the bottom. Thea screamed again through her gag, the sound emerging as a high pitched squeal.

The killer stepped back and took in his handiwork. The ends of the girl's fabulous breasts were an angry red, swollen from their abuse. Her distended legs were twitching from the pain in her sex. Her eyes recorded her torment, spread wide and filled with the waters of her tears. She was a pretty picture. He stepped closer to her and grabbed her teats, wrenching them cruelly. Thea sobbed and tried to twist her torso away from his iron grip. He held her still, watching the anguish rise up in the girl's pretty, blue eyes. Of course he would start with the tits. Wasn't that what anyone would do?

Drabik released the sobbing girl's nipples and went back to his trunk. He retrieved a whip with a stout, leather encased handle and seven two foot long, thick, leather tassels. The ends were knotted and had been soaked in vinegar, making them stiff and hard. He gripped the heinous instrument in his strong right arm and approached his victim.

He had not spoken to her since her had returned to the tent. There was not much to say. But now he wanted to measure the girl's fear, heighten it, taunt her helplessness. "I think that you're going to enjoy this, little slave girl," he told her maliciously, dragging the stiff knots of the whip across her alabaster breasts. "Your pretty breasts will soon be criss-crossed with dark red welts. All of the slave girls love it. It's their favorite whip."

Thea moaned as she took in the tool of her upcoming torture. "...eeeeeease on't!" she whined miserably, looking up desperately at her tormentor. "....eeeeeease!" she repeated. Panicked, she tried to pull her chest away from contact with the foul implement, but she had nowhere to go.

Drabik laughed at her obsequiousness. "I'm afraid I have to little slave girl," he returned to her. "Your mounds are just so pretty and defenseless. They're just begging to be abused. If you didn't want to be whipped, you shouldn't have grown such wonderful tits."

That was exactly how Thea was feeling right then. She cursed the fate that had decreed that her womanly growths should be so round and heavy, that spread her areolas across their tops so widely and invitingly. She would have given anything at this moment to have them small, petite, unnoticeable. She would have given anything to be anywhere else in the world rather than be trussed and vulnerable in this madman's tent.

The madman reached his arm back taking the whip with it. He unleashed it at the girl's swaying, red tipped mammaries. The thick tassels flew across her pale flesh, the knots gorged deep grooves in it, leaving behind a trail of rising red.

"Aaaaaaaauuuuuuuugh!" Thea cried out. Even the thick leather in her mouth could not mask entirely her anguished wail. "Ohhhhhhhh! Ohhhhhhhhhh!" she moaned.

Drabik waited until the effects of the blow had fully sunk into the girl's being. The left breast, which had received the brunt of the vicious attack, was lined with long, reddish streaks. The killer shifted hands and delivered a blow from left to right and the girl's right breast was marked to match the other. "Aaaaaaauuuuuugh! Aaaaauuu-uuugh! …eeeease! …eeeeeeease op! …eeeeease!" she yelled as her body writhed in agony.

Her torturer ignored her pleas. Methodically, his rage building higher and higher even as he tried to exorcize it, he attacked the girl's femininity. Cursing the fate that had entangled him in an obsessive morass for the brown tailed ponygirl, Lightning, he laid the whip across the sides, the tops, the bottom and even in between the girl's dancing, heaving orbs. When he struck them dead across the nipples was when he drew the most piteous wails from her, the already sensitized teats radiating agony through the girl's voluptuous body.

Drabik, sweating and panting from his evil efforts, paused to take in the artwork of his anger. The girl's large, round breasts were not so pretty any more. Long, deep maroon lines crossed them this way and that. Here and there, small drops of blood were oozing from the lacerations. He knew that he needed to move on lest he damage the orbs permanently.

He stooped down and joined the girl's ankles together. The girl barely registered his action being lost in a haze of unbearable pain. She awoke right enough when he brought the whip across her flat, smooth belly. He struck her thighs, her shins and her belly again and again. Moving to her back, he grew deep red trails across her flesh there, across her plump, pale white rump and the back of her legs.

Thea's screams went on and on. When the cruel man paused, her cries morphed into deep, mournful wails and sobs. Her eyes looked at him piteously, seeking some shred of mercy. Her face was slick with her tears and sweat teemed down her torso from her armpits and her chest.

Little was left of the girl's tender aspect when Drabik finally finished with her. She swayed back and forth on the chain that held her hands high above her and continued a low, mournful moan. Drabik tossed the whip aside. He reached above her and unfastened the chain from her wrist bracelets. The girl collapsed to the floor.

His cock was hard and needy. Stripping his clothes from his body, he knelt next to the girl. She was balled into a little circle, sobbing. No one had whipped her like that since the horrid, initial days of her slave training. All the things that the other slave girls had said about the man were true. Her eyes jammed shut, sensing the naked body of her assailant next to her, she prayed that he had no new, more agonizing torments in store.

Drabik pushed the girl to her back and released her ankles from each other. Her slit was still clamped tightly closed. When he tore off the cruel implements from her love lips, Thea screamed with pain. The clamps had left deep gauges in the sides of her tender labia. She automatically pulled her knees up to her chest in reaction. Drabik placed his hands on her bruised legs, forced them back down again and then insinuated himself between her battered thighs. She looked up at him, her body shivering with fear. She felt his hand prying at her sex. Trying desperately to make herself ready for his assault in accordance with her training, she attempted to recall better times with real lovers. She could not get the violence with which the man had whipped her out of her head, nor the stinging ache from her bruised love lips. His fingers rubbed against her point of pleasure and her slice began to lubricate in self defense. When she felt his fingers slide inside her, she thanked the heavens for this small mercy.

The fevered ponygirl trainer rubbed his stiff cock the length of the girl's crevasse, dipping its fat head in her growing moisture. Slowly, he eased himself forward, plunging into her hole. Her cunt was hot, almost feverish, after her travail. Her whole body was hot from its abuse. Drabik took the girl's still bound hands and raised them over her head. He pressed his chest against hers and began to rock his hips. His tempo increased rapidly. His lust was upon him. The vision of the girl's gagged mouth, her frightened, anguished eyes, drove his passions higher and higher. The blood from her wounds smeared onto his body as he pumped back and forth rapidly in her conch, slamming his hips against hers and making her moan. When he came, he yelled his anger out, "Aaaaaaarrrrrrrgh! Aaaaaaaarrrrrrrgh!" while his creamy discharge flooded the girl's womb. She cried out behind her gag in fear and unhappiness. In all her three years as a slave girl, she had never been fucked with such fury. He was truly a madman. She prayed that after he had achieved his delight, he would finally let her go.

When his cock ceased its pulsing in the girl's pussy, Drabik rolled off of her and onto his back. "That's better," he thought. His anger had dissipated for now. Leaving the sobbing girl where she lay, he stood and grabbed a towel to wipe her blood from his body. "She was a tasty morsel," he thought. He felt like going out for a few drinks. One of the estates was going to have a performance of dancing slave girls and he did not want to miss it.

Quickly, he redonned his clothes. He went over to the now quiet and limp girl and prodded her in the side with his foot. "Roll over," he told her. Thea gave a great sob as she realized that her ordeal was not yet over. Fearful of worsening his wrath, she obeyed and was soon lying on her belly.

Taking the chain which had recently suspended the girl in his hands, he looped it through the linked rings in her connected wrist bracelets. He then pulled her arms back over her head, making her back arch painfully.

"Ooooooooouuuuuuu!" the girl moaned as her shoulder muscles began to ache terribly. Drabik turned and, grabbing one ankle, slid the chain through the ring in her ankle bracelet. He repeated the exercise with the other and then pulled the chain tight until the girl's feet were in the air behind her nearly meeting her stretched out hands. He slid the chain once more through her wrist rings and then clipped it off so that it would hold her limbs in place. He then pulled on the free end until the girl's arms and legs were strained upwards and the only contact she had with the ground was her tortured belly and her wounded teats.

Thea moaned disconsolately. Drabik put on his heavy, black boots and then went over to his demonic trunk. He returned with a thick, leather encased riding crop in his hand. He crouched down next to the girl and placed it on the ground before her. "I'm going out for a while," he told her. "I need to relax. When I come back, we'll get to work again. While I'm gone, I want you to keep an eye on my riding crop and think about the many ways I can hurt you with it."

Chuckling to himself, he got up and left the tent.

CHAPTER FIVE

On the second morning of the tournament, Lightning was awoken early by her slave girl attendant. After her ritual shavings and feeding, she was bathed and refitted with a new, clean hood. Jerzi was up too and he took the time to allow her a short while to suck on his cock before having her harnessed and affixed to her cart for her morning run.

There were not so many teams in the tournament as yesterday and it was easier to find adequate room for exercising the pony's sleep laden legs. When they returned to the encampment, the slave girl, Amanda, brought her close to orgasm several times with her mouth while they waited for the doctor to appear and examine her foot.

Yesterday, Lightning had had three races. The first two were perfunctory, being against ponies with low seeds. The third was the closest to a real race as she battled against the number five seed pony. When she pulled into her victory lap, Jerzi detected a distinct limp in her right foot. Once back at the encampment, he had the foot iced for a long time to reduce the swelling.

Lightning's first race was around ten. She was to go against the number three seed, a pony who had won a good number of races and to whom Lightning had actually lost in the second race of the season. Lightning was new to the 3000 meter race at that point and her record improved steadily after that. But so did the other pony's. Her three losses were once against the number two seed in the tournament and twice under severe weather conditions. Unlike yesterday, Lightning would today be faced with a series of real races.

The doctor came around about 8:30. Lightning was kneeling in the grass, her right boot off awaiting his inspection. He took a good look at the foot, moving it this way and that and then applied some more antiseptic cream to her wound.

"I don't like it," he told Jerzi in Russian. "It's definitely weaker than yesterday. I think that she's been running more on the side of her foot and that's creating a whole new tension. If it were up to me, I'd send her home right now."

"Well, it's not up to you," Jerzi told him. "Just do your job and keep your mouth shut. If she gets disqualified because of her foot, before Grobgy kills me, I'll hunt you down and slit your throat. Got it?"

Unused to such suggestions of direct violence against his person, the doctor blanched. "Of course I'll say nothing," he answered. He wondered whether all this tension was worth the substantial sum he was paid to attend to the health of the ponygirls. There were the prerequisites of his position though. He also took care of the pretty and sexually available slave girls and often got his dick wet. He was going to have to give this a lot of thought when his contract came up again.

Both Grobgy and Drabik made visits to the campsite, although at different times. Grobgy stayed for coffee and a blowjob from Amanda. The pretty, black haired, British slave girl hoped that her efforts would please him and yet not be so good as to make him want her to be assigned to him again once the tournament was over.

Drabik's visit was quicker. He demanded to know what the doctor had said. "Then why are we racing her?" he wanted to know when he was told of the wear on her foot. Jerzi shrugged his shoulders and told him to go ask Axmail Grobgy.

At 9:30, Lightning was reharnessed and hooked up to her cart. As usual, Jerzi left Amanda bound and gagged in the campsite. He gave her an affectionate pat on the head before leaving. She had shown much promise lately and had not gotten lost when retrieving his meals since the first day.

When they arrived at the track, a pair of mighty landau teams were rumbling along its dirt surface. Jerzi paused his pony at the entrance gate to watch them. He was too small to ever handle a team like that, but he envied the drivers of such powerful ponies. The grass is always greener on the other side of the fence and many of the other drivers wished that they were small enough to drive the sleek speedsters of the sport.

When the landau race was completed, Jerzi pulled Lightning onto the track for an additional warm up lap even while the landaus were doing their cool downs. The other team came onto the dirt track as well. The pony wore an all red hood and its cart was bedecked with red and white ribbons. The emblem of the estate, a snarling jackal on a sea of red was emblazoned on a pennant that sailed behind the cart as it ran and on the ponygirl's flat, taut, belly.

Jerzi had given some thought as to his strategy. As he had predicted, in her early races the opposing drivers had gone all out at the beginning of the race hoping to capitalize on Lightning's vulnerability. It hadn't worked so far. Those were ponies of somewhat lesser light than Lightning although they were good enough to make the tournament. This pony was much closer to Lightning's class. If Lighting had not been injured, he would have no worries. She could finish the other pony off easily. It already had one loss, to the second seed pony, and one more would put it out of the tournament.

The vast majority of drivers would have assumed that this pony would follow the same strategy as the others. But Jerzi had guessed differently. He believed that since Lightning had proven she could go wire to wire at near top speed, this driver would try and slow the race down and then make a mad dash to the finish line in the hopes that Lightning's injury would prevent her from accelerating fast enough to catch him. Jerzi had his own plan for how to deal with that.

The two ponies lined up at the start and waited for the gun to sound. The other pony, whose name was Felisa, Spanish for Lucky, reflecting her heritage, was from Aliseda, a small town not too far from the Portuguese border. Her father had run, ironically enough, a pony ranch there. The region was dry and dusty and no place for a lovely, broad shouldered and tall, randy 19 year old to find excitement. One of the migrant hands her father had hired for the calving season, a dark Basque with an adventurous, black moustache and a certain way about him, had seduced her and convinced her to run away with him to Barcelona. They went to Barcelona all right, but their destination was not some romantic hotel overlooking the Mediterranean, but a run down warehouse in the industrial section of the city. There she was held prisoner for three days, servicing the men who stripped and bound her, and then flown with three other beauties to Kalikastan. Like all the other ponies, she had cried and moaned when she was dehumanized and went through the same tortuous training during which all thoughts of return to a normal life had been beaten out of her. Now, two years later, she was a sleek, muscular, dark skinned pony ready to move up to a championship if things just fell her way.

You did not get up to championship class without being a hard, determined pony. Felisa, unlucky enough to have fallen for a bastard like Ambroso, the cowboy, had been luckier in her trainer who had been bringing her along the last two years. She was now at her peak. If she did not champion this year, she might run as a sulky for a few more seasons but would then be either converted to one of the larger teams, probably the four pony broughams whose carriage tended to be lighter than the larger teams', or farmed out to one of the lesser estates where the owners would run her purely for pleasure and prestige purposes.

And so, the match between Lightning and Felisa promised to be an interesting race. Felisa's driver would be desperate for a win and would drive the pony hard. Lightning was still suffering from her injury. Jerzi was not the only one to notice her limp after her last race yesterday and to realize that it needed to be nursed along until the finals.

The grandstands were full and betting was heavy. It was another beautiful, fall day. The pennants above the grandstands flapped noisily like crow's wings in the breeze. A hush came over the crowd as the two ponygirls were led to the start line by their drivers.

Jake was watching from the grandstands with Irkut. He had not seen Tanya yet this morning. Last night, he had wandered aimlessly among the parties and the slave girl shows, disjointed and ill at ease. So much was riding on such a slender thread. Maybe it had been a foolish idea to bring Jackie all the way over here and put her whole life at risk for Maddy. In the end, what did it matter to him whether Burnham's niece ever was liberated? Everyone was somebody's daughter or son and he had seen plenty of unfortunate, enslaved, young women whose lives were just as important to them as Maddy's presumably was to hers. He rued the fact that he had had a hand in bringing so many of them to Kalikastan, not to mention laying the groundwork for the toxic mix of Burnham's millions and the ruthlessness of the Russians who ran this place.

Jake had walked out to the public area of the fairgrounds to mingle with the plebian campers there. Men and women sat around campfires drinking and reliving the day's great races. His Russian was elementary, but he heard Chocolate's Russian name mentioned several times. Here and there a bedraggled slave girl hustled to deliver this or that to the campers. He saw several on their knees either on all fours receiving a thick cock between her thighs or servicing a besotted racing fan with her mouth.

These were not the beautiful, almost pristine slave girls you found on the wealthy estates or in the boudoirs of fancy whorehouses. These were girls who had already spent considerable time 'under the collar', as they called it, and had descended the ladder a rung or two. In a few years, or maybe sooner, most of them would find their way to the lesser whorehouses or serving drunken louts in blood and beer taverns. This was the underside of Kalikastan that Irkut didn't talk about.

He recalled, as he walked along, the elegant, refined beauty of the ponygirl specialist, Dr. Kevsky, and her soft demeanor and tender hands as she worked Chocolate's puss. Her civilized, caring aspect was belied by the fact that she supported and encouraged a cruel system of human slavery. He wondered what horrors the young girls who were brought to her experimental facility had to bear. She said her methods were harsh but yielded good results. But good for whom? And for her to describe her methods as harsh spoke volumes. For any Kalikastani to consider something harsh as it applied to slave girls, it had to be way beyond the pale.

His thoughts also turned to the beautiful and delightful Tanya. Part of him wanted to chuck everything aside and give himself over to her. She said that her father could use someone like him. He could walk up to Burnham this very night and tell him to go fuck himself. But where would that leave Jackie, who was depending on him to free her? What about his resolution to save Maddy? And even Tanya's delightful, playful presence was marred by her devotion to the national sport and her ambition to train her own ponygirls.

He had done some terrible things in the course of pursuing Maddy's freedom. But perhaps, if she were liberated, she would serve as some kind of symbol of freedom, belie the expression he had heard so many times, "Once a ponygirl, always a ponygirl." Jake was no crusader, but maybe he could bring about just a small leak in the country's system of female slavery that could cause an eventual flood.

He strolled by the now empty and moonlit fields where they had held the show pony demonstrations. He recalled the ethereal beauty of the slender, graceful ponygirls with the lavender hoods. There was something about them that made his heart ache. Not because they were poor, unfortunate females once accepted as human beings who now led cruel lives under deplorable restraints. That would have been understandable, acceptable.

No, it was that he appreciated their captive beauty. In this, Irkut was right. Where else could such a thing be possible? True, the lives of two young women had been sacrificed to create this wondrous image of the hooded, bound and bitted ponygirls dancing lightly, unashamed at their nakedness, happy to please the salacious interests of the crowd. He doubted that any cock was left unstirred, that no pussy failed to moisten as the sensuous creatures ran through their routines. He knew that his libido was sharpened by the sight and the thought of their sexuality. He knew that their delicate, hairless pussies were subject to relentless plowing, that their mouths had encircled countless cocks, and yet, to him, they had preserved their innocent, beauteous aspects.

Was the esthetic pleasure that the show ponies brought worth the travail that the ponygirls suffered? Who could say? Decisions were made every day all over the globe that effected the well being and lives of millions. Toxic pollutants permeate the atmosphere so that we can drive to the beach when we want to. Benign creatures of the earth like the whales were sacrificed so that we could have make-up and cat food. How many Congolese died every year so that the rapacious corporations of the west could process their mineral wealth for the benefit of beer guzzling Westerners? Were the millions who died under Stalin's reign justified by the rise in fortunes of the average Russian? What about the Chinese who now possessed one of the most dynamic economies on the globe as a result of years of oppression? When we take in the grandeur of the Pyramids or the Coliseum in Rome, do we shout, "Take them down!" because they were built by slave labor and many hundreds or even thousands of people died so that they could be built? Is Caesar considered any less great in bringing Roman civilization to the rest of Western Europe by the fact that he slaughtered hundreds of thousands of Gauls and other 'barbarians' during his conquests?

Jake was no philosopher. He could not answer such questions. It was not up to him to say what, in the vast scheme of things, was right or wrong. What he did know was that it was wrong to break his word. He had given his pledge to save Maddy and that's what he would do. He had promised Jackie that he would bring her out, and that's what he would do. He would leave the poisoned paradise of Kalikastan behind forever.

When Jake arrived back at the trailer that he and Burnham shared, it was very late. The revelers had mostly gone to bed. He had passed a tent in which some slave girl was being brought to an ecstatic series of orgasms. Her guttural cries of pleasure echoed through the otherwise silent night. Burnham had already gone to bed. He had apparently found another bedmate since the Malaysian girl was still in her cage. The birdlike Betty was there too, fast asleep, her plastic orange beak covering her mouth, her arms bound behind her. The third cage was empty. Apparently someone had decided that the pretty slave girl who called the small, steel confinement home would serve as his lascivious entertainment tonight.

Jake tapped on the cage of the Malaysian girl, Orchid. She awoke with a start. Her eyes darted about her frantically. When she saw that it was him, her tension eased. A faint light shined in through the windows of the otherwise dark trailer and Jake thought that he saw her face smile. He gestured to her as if asking her if he should release her from her cage and she nodded her agreement. She was gagged and had her arms bound behind her. Jake opened the cage and let the girl crawl out. When she stood, the moonlight glinted off of her smooth, delicate skin. Her breasts quivered. She followed Jake's lead willingly as he brought her into his room. He released her arms from behind her back and removed her gag. When her body was unrestricted, he pulled her onto the bed and, while she waited expectantly, removed his clothes.

Jake crept onto the bed and placed his hands on the girl's cheeks. He kissed her tenderly and drew her body to his. He lay back, taking her with him.

The couple lay there in the bed silently for a long while. Jake could hear the deep, steady breathing of the girl and feel the beating of her heart against his chest. He had just started to nod off when he felt the girl's hand wander across it. The small hand ran over his belly and then her lips delicately pressed against his skin. He had had no carnal intent when he had freed the girl from her tiny confines. He just wanted to alleviate her suffering for one night, let her feel human again. As her hand wandered his body and her lips grazed along his skin, he felt his resolution not to make use of her slipping away.

The naked, dark skinned, beautiful Malaysian girl rose from her supine position and straddled him. Her body was hot and smooth. She leaned over and placed her lips on his. Her tongue slid out languorously, teased his oral opening and then darted inside. Her breasts lay mashed against his chest and her thighs gripped his hips tightly. Jake gave a deep sigh and placed his arms around her.

They kissed for a long time. Jake's mind was overwhelmed with passion. Every time the girl moved, as she ground her soft, hairless pussy against his belly, or pressed her breasts hard against him, she sent an intense thrill throughout his body.

Jake made a move to turn the girl onto her back so that he could possess her. She pressed back against him and whispered, "No, please, Master." She lifted her leg over his torso and, placing her gentle hands underneath him and said, "Please, Master, please."

Surprised at the girl's forwardness, Jake let her turn him to his belly. She climbed atop him once more and began to stroke the well defined muscles of his back and shoulders while pressing her lips and tongue against him.

The strength of the girl's fingers belied her apparent fragility. She seemed to know where every muscle started and ended. Jake groaned as she massaged him. She followed each pleasurable manipulation of his flesh with a kiss from her hot lips and a caress from her agile tongue. She moved down his torso and massaged his thighs and the back of his shins. She dragged her small, firm beasts against him everywhere she went and let her long, black hair slide sensuously over his skin. When she had finished with his legs, she brought her attentions back up again, teasing and massaging each of his vertebrae, covering every inch of his back with her knowledgeable caresses.

Jake was lost in a heavenly reverie. Although his cock was hard as a rock, he had almost slipped off into a relaxing sleep when Orchid urged him to turn on his back. Once he had complied with her wishes, she commenced the same treatment to his chest and the front of his thighs as she had his other side. She worked the muscles of his shoulders and his trim, taut pectorals. As she slid down him, she seized his nipples and sucked at them hard, causing him to groan. Her delicate hands fluttered across his thighs and hips.

The girl's adorations to his body had caused his cock to stand straight up. She studiously avoided it during her initial ministrations to his flesh, but when she had done his thighs and his muscular chest once more, she took hold of the solid shaft with her dainty hand. Jake sighed as he felt her warmth transferred to his manhood. Her breasts slid across his belly, the firm points dragging across his skin. And then she took possession of him with her mouth.

His body was so relaxed that the tension in his cock seemed almost anomalous. His being seemed to swirl around it as the moist heat of the girl's mouth and the delectable pressure that she brought to bear with her busy tongue and lips created a whirlpool of lust in him. Her hand gently stroked his shaft as her mouth subsumed his fleshy helmet and her tongue swished over the sensitive glans. She moved her head up and down slowly as if her attentions to his needy prick could last all night. Certainly Jake wished that they could. She had brought him to a state bordering bliss. All his worries, all his uncertainties slipped away.

The beautiful Malaysian girl's passion inducing attentions to his body were, he realized, her unsolicited response to his gesture of warmth to her. In a land filled with cruelty, a small act of kindness was magnified far beyond its normal significance. She was giving back to him in return the only thing that she had to give, her ability to drive his lusts and to pleasure his body. He lifted his hand and languorously stroked her smooth, jet black hair as an expression of his appreciation of her gratitude. He moaned as her mouth descended his pole, driving its tip into her slender, narrow throat and back again. He felt his balls tightening and his climax approaching. She detected the imminence of his explosion and her mouth increased its energetic pleasuring of his sex. When his orgasm came, he issued a deep, appreciative groan. His fluid pumped out of him in intense, body shaking spurts. Orchid drank it down like it was ambrosia. He heard her give out a little moan of her own as his passionate explosion reverberated in her own lust.

Once his cock had given all that it had to give, the girl rubbed her hands over his belly and the insides of his thighs. He went to pull her up so that he could express his appreciation of her gift of herself to him, but she resisted, holding his hands off. Her mouth had not let go of his meaty wand. Her tongue and lips still worked it lovingly. She removed them only to devote attention to his well satisfied sac. She gently massaged his stones with her tongue while sucking softly on the tender enclosure, her hand deftly exercising his still tumescent shaft.

Jake felt his cock springing back to life. He was no superman, but he was used to achieving sexual release four or five times a day since he had become a resident in this carnal paradise. He had not achieved orgasm since the late morning when he and Tanya had made love on this very bed. It was not surprising that his reserves had not been exhausted.

Orchid returned her mouth to his cock and gave it several loving strokes with her lips. His manhood had achieved rigidity once more. This time, she released the stiff shaft and moved her body upwards. She let her tongue drift across his belly and chest until her loins were poised over his. She had possession of his prick in her hand and she aimed it at her moistened slit. Slowly, once its head had pierced its outer opening, she lowered herself onto him, impaling herself.

A wave of delight passed over him. She placed her hands on his chest and began to rock slowly back and forth, giving his cock loving caresses with the tender walls of her quim. After a while, she leaned over and kissed his chest, shifting herself, but keeping his rigid pole prisoner in her cleft.

Jake knew that the girl was intent on receiving her own, very deserved pleasure. He wondered whether she was recalling, physically and mentally, a lover from her past, maybe even her recent past, since she had been a slave girl only little more than two weeks. That she had had at least one devoted lover there was no doubt from her skillful pleasuring of him. Jake opened his eyes and took in her dreamy countenance lit by the yellow light of the almost full moon through the window in his room. She was somewhere else, there was no doubt about that. Some men would have been offended that their cocks did not hold the woman's full attention, but Jake knew better. Stolen from her life, what right did Jake have to deny her a few moments of return to a more happy state? As far as he was concerned, she could do it every time.

The delicate, brown skinned girl spent a long time caressing his manhood with her hot cleft. Twice, she slowed the graceful, deliberate movements of her hips and he felt her body tense, heard her moan. Her body shook as she received her own pleasure. When her orgasm had passed, she began her movements once again.

Having come just a few minutes before, Jake's cock had plenty of stamina to give to the impassioned girl. He rocked his hips back against her, careful to match her rhythms, to let her dictate the pace of their coitus. When he could resist it no longer and after, by his count, the girl had experienced three mesmerizing effusions of lust, he increased his pace. The girl picked up on his signal and began to stroke his cock energetically with her puss. Her heat surrounded his cock and the passion inducing friction of her soft interior was delivering ecstatic sensations to his brain. He heard her moan and gasp as her climax overtook her. Her hips still pumping at his loins, she bent her head down and took possession of his lips. They kissed madly as their mutual explosions of pleasure heightened each other's delight. Jake moaned and groaned as his cock spewed forth his essence, Orchid sighed and cried out as her pussy delivered to him the effects of her intense, hard, contractions.

As must always happen, their passions finally ebbed. Jake felt an overwhelming sense of tenderness for the female who had brought him such pleasure. He didn't know what her thoughts were, but he knew that her body had produced a surfeit of pleasure to her, the only reward a slave girl can really have. She slowed and then ceased her rocking motions on his cock and let her body slump against his. Jake's body felt limp and weak. He caught himself drifting off to a zone of satisfaction. But he had one more favor to do the poor, little Malaysian girl. He gently moved her body off of his and lay her down on her back. He took hold of her hands and locked her wrist bands together and then connected them to a chain that led from the headboard of his bed.

He had no idea whether the girl would get it in her mind to try and escape. He didn't care if she did, as long as she was not caught. He had seen the results of retribution on the bodies of slave girls who had run away and it was not pleasant. Although he knew of the virtual impossibility of escape, she undoubtedly did not. So clipping her wrists and keeping her prisoner in his bed was, ironically, an act of kindness towards her. She looked at him with unhappiness but was quickly brought back to acceptance of the need to confine her. He placed his arm around her shoulders, drawing her body against his once more, kissed her, and then fell asleep.

* * * * * * * * * * * * * *

As Jake watched the two ponies line up for their race the next morning, he had a moment's recollection of his evening with the Malaysian slave girl and smiled to himself. He was a fool. All it took was the sight of a delectable body and he was off to the races. His pretensions of morality and ethics was a paper construct, to be dashed at the first opportunity.

He looked out at the wonderful flesh poised at the start line. He let his binoculars bring him inches away from their hairless divides, their blooming breasts. Who was he kidding? He was going to miss Kalikastan.

The gun sounded and the ponies were off.

Felisa's driver started her out slow. Lightning was surprised that her driver did not take advantage of her torpid pace to put some distance between them. She did not take it upon herself to question his strategy. He knew his business as her prior races with him had proven again and again.

Felisa's driver was confused. He had expected Lightning to drive hard to gain a large lead. His strategy was to lay just behind her, just enough to deny her the inside rail. When they reached the ¾ pole on the second lap, he would whip his pony into the sprint of her life. Jerzi was not taking the bait. He was handling Lightning as if he were on a Sunday drive. Each time, however, the other driver tried to get the lead on Jerzi's pony, he would increase her pace so that he kept just ahead of him. It was his strategy in reverse.

The ponies were still in the same position when they finished their first lap. There were some catcalls from the stands, remarking on the torpid pace that the ponies were maintaining. The opinions of the crowd, however, have no place in strategy to a good ponygirl driver and both men were among the best.

Suddenly, as the two ponies crossed the half way mark of the second and final lap, Jerzi gave Lightning's reins a heavy snap. Lightning leapt into action instantaneously. Felisa's driver was taken wholly by surprise. The brown tailed pony wasn't supposed to have this in her because of her injured foot. It took him a few, fateful seconds to react. By that time, Lightning was gone.

The energized pony put all that she had into her long dash to the finish line. Jake and Irkut stood up, as did most of the crowd. "I don't believe it," Irkut said. "If she pulls this off, she deserves the gold medal. That's a long way to sprint. I hope that she has it in her."

Jake nervously took in the drama unfolding before him. Lightning's lead quickly spread to two lengths. The red hooded pony had recovered and was digging its boots frantically into the dirt to catch up. Ponytails were flying in the wind, whips were cracking. The crowd held its breath. Would Lightning fade? Would her foot give out? Could the fast, black tailed pony catch her?

The two fine animals raced towards the finish line. Felisa was slowly closing the gap. But Jerzi had one more surprise. Lightning had not become a champion by chance or luck. She had a deep well of spirit in her that needed to win, needed to excel. When the ponies were a mere 50 yards away from the finish line, Jerzi gave the reins one more crack.

Lightning was deeply involved in the single minded mechanics of putting one boot before the other. She had the focus and intensity of a champion. Yet, she was also superbly trained, totally committed to obedience. She had thought she was giving all that she could give. Her lungs were near bursting and her thighs were feeling the strain. She was wrong. When she felt the command of her driver transferred down the length of her reins for one more intense burst of speed, she obeyed without question. No thought precipitated her reaction. Her body and spirit knew what to do.

The crowd drew its breath in awe as Lightning suddenly pulled ahead of the red hooded pony once more. It was if the black tailed pony's driver had put on the brakes. When Lightning crossed the finish line, she had a good ¾'s length lead.

"I'll be damned," Irkut said as the tall, broad shouldered, big breasted pony entered her victory lap. He tore up his ducats and tossed them into the air. It seemed that even one of the foremost experts on ponygirls could be wrong once in a while. As usual, Jake had put his money on Lightning and was smiling. "I'll buy you a drink," he told Irkut.

"Buy me one too while you're at it," a cocky, female voice called out. It was Tanya and she was smiling broadly. "How's Chocolate," she asked when she sat down next to Jake.

Jake was surprised at how happy he was to see her. He had dreaded meeting up with her since he had avoided going to her mother's campsite last night even though he could have. It was that woman spurned thing. But she, apparently, had no resentment at his exercise in independence.

Jake signaled a passing slave girl and ordered a gin and tonic for himself. It was too early for straight gin. Irkut ordered a tall, dark ale and Tanya asked for a Cube Libré. "I'm not much of a drinker in the morning," she said by way of apology.

"And what have you been up to this morning," Jake asked her.

"I've been helping mama with the ponies." She lifted her hand to Jake's nose. It was covered with the pungent aroma of female arousal. "You should have come over last night, Jake. Mama keeps her ponygirls very passionate. Molly missed you."

Jake laughed. "I'm sure someone made up for my absence," he replied.

Their drinks were delivered. Jake handed the slave girl a wad of zlotskis and she stuffed them into the cloth pouch she wore around her waist. It was probably the closest thing to clothing she had worn in a long time.

"You didn't answer me," Tanya said as Jake and Irkut took gulps from their drinks. "How's Chocolate?"

Jake and Irkut had visited Chocolate's campsite at first light. Dr. Kevsky had spent the night with her. When they entered the encampment, she was lying on her side next to the ponygirl, her mouth on Chocolate's breast and her hand in her quim. Chocolate was moaning and grinding her booted heels in the grass. Her explosion came just as the men came near her.

"Mmmmmmmmmmpf! Mmmmmmmmmmmpf!" she moaned through her gag. She shook her hooded head back and forth. Perspiration beaded all over her chocolate colored body. It seemed that Dr. Kevsky had been tormenting the pony's cleft for a long time and had finally permitted her release.

"I hope you never do that to me," Jake quipped when the ponygirl physician rose to her feet.

"Oh yes you do, Jake," she returned. "And as soon as Tanya gives me permission, I will."

Her blouse was open and one of her lovely breasts was peaking out. Ilona, Giorgi's slave girl was kneeling expectantly in the grass next to Chocolate. Giorgi was sitting in his chair morosely drinking coffee.

"Come here, Ilona," the doctor instructed.

The blond slave girl jumped to her feet and scurried over. Dr. Kevsky stroked her hair gently. "I want you to make Chocolate come one more time. Do it like I showed you," she told her. "Make her last at least fifteen minutes, okay?"

"Yes, Mistress," Ilona answered. She seemed eager to please the tall, blond doctor. Jake noticed that she had several red stripes across her breasts. Kevsky observed Jake looking at them.

"Ilona and I had a little misunderstanding when I came here last night," she told Jake. "But I think we straightened it out. Isn't that so, Ilona?"

"Yes, Mistress," the girl replied happily as if being whipped made everything crystal clear.

Jake was taken aback once more at the doctor's ability to mix cruelty with her gentleness. The woman slid her hand behind Ilona's head and pulled her to her breast. Ilona gave out an impassioned sigh and took the doctor's teat in her mouth. As she sucked on it earnestly, Svetlana caressed her breast in return. She closed her eyes, reveling in the girl's oral attentions. After a few moments, she eased Ilona's head away from her chest and took possession of her lips with her own. Jake's cock stirred as he watched the two blond women, one free, one slave, engage in a lustful exchange of tongue. Both he and Irkut were mesmerized. When the women broke their kiss, both of their eyes soft and glassy, their chests rising and falling in deep breaths, Svetlana urged the slave girl to her task. She turned to the men while tucking her breast back into her white blouse and said, "Would you like some coffee?"

Jake tried to hide his erection as he sat down near the campfire while the doctor poured him a cup of the thick, black brew.

"I think she'll be okay," the physician said. "I understand that her first race will not be a serious challenge but that depending on how the other races go, her second may be more difficult."

"Since she ran four races yesterday, the most that she'll have to run today is three, in all probability," Irkut added.

"Three is still a lot," Jake said as he blew on the steaming cup.

The doctor and the ponygirl expert conveyed their agreement with Jake's statement by their silence.

"Maybe she'll get lucky," Irkut said after a while.

"If she makes it through today, she'll be even stronger tomorrow," Svetlana offered. "We just have to take it one step at a time."

Jake could not take his eyes off of the arcs of the doctor's mammaries revealed by her only partially buttoned blouse. Where did all these randy women come from, he wondered. It did make sense though. If the men had the opportunity to satisfy their sexual urges virtually whenever and however they pleased, the women had limited choices in response. They could engage in a fruitless campaign to bring the men to heel, that was one option. Another was that they could retire to their tents and be good little housewives, suffering in passive aggressiveness. Some of the women, he had noticed, engaged in a form of heightened femininity, wearing elaborate coiffures, elegant dresses, long, virtually handicapping nails. Helena, her daughter and Dr. Kevsky had chosen a fourth path. If you could not beat the men, why not join them? If the men could engage in displays of untrammeled eroticism, why not the women?

It was somewhat off-putting to a social conservative like Jake, but he sensed it was something he could get used to. Kalikastan was a mad, mad, mad, mad world. If the whole world was crazy, the rational would seem insane. Everything that Jake had thought about sexuality, all of his sexual mores, had gone by the boards long ago. In fact, the entire premise of sexual slavery and ponygirls was that females were not beings to coddle and treat with gentlemanly deference. Exactly the opposite. There was little difference between the women natives of Kalikastan and the women who served there as slaves other than the accident of birth and being in the wrong place at the wrong time. If some women were considered as virulently sexual, why not all women? He had to admit that Dr. Kevsky's frank sexual aggressiveness turned him on.

Jake looked over at Giorgi. The driver seemed depressed. He would need to snap out of it if her were to be any help to Chocolate. It must be disconcerting to him to have the female doctor take over his sexual dominance of the pony, Jake figured. Well, he would have to get over it.

A deep, virtually anguished groan from Chocolate turned all of their heads. She was writhing in the grass as Ilona suckled on one of her deliciously formed breasts while her hand tantalized her quim. Jake guessed that it was about fifteen minutes. Ilona released Chocolate's stiff, fat nipple from her mouth and looked at Svetlana. The doctor nodded. Ilona went back to her work with alacrity, sucking intently on the pony's tit while grinding her fingers in her luscious crevasse. Chocolate raised her knees and groaned as her orgasm commenced. Ilona's hand kept up its teasing of her twat as the pony shuddered and groaned. After a long forty seconds or so, the equine female gave out a long, grateful sigh. Ilona looked up at Dr. Kevsky and smiled.

The doctor turned back to Jake and Irkut. "She's such a delightful slave girl," she said.

Irkut leaned over and whispered to her, "She's for sale, you know."

"Ohhhhhh," the woman said pensively. She looked back at the blond slave girl who was cuddling with the satisfied, brown skinned pony.

"Twenty thousand zlotskis," Irkut said lowly.

She looked back at the men. "I'll have to give it some thought."

"How are Helena's ponies doing," Jake asked. "You've spent so much time here, doesn't she need you?"

"I stopped over last night. One of the ponies, Fiona, had a slight sprain to her ankle, but I think she'll be all right. I iced it up and gave her a muscle relaxant."

Jake wondered if the doctor meant with her hand.

He looked over at Chocolate. "Won't all this relaxing make it difficult for her to get up for her race?" he asked her.

"Well, it is a problem, but you can't have one without the other. I'll give her a few solid strokes of the whip across her breasts about a half hour before race time," she said. "That should get her blood up."

Jake nodded. It would wake him up.

"We missed you last night Jake," she said. "Tanya was forlorn without you."

"I don't think I would have been very good company," he replied. "I needed to work some things out."

"We all hope you give Tanya a chance," the doctor added. "She's really fallen for you and she needs someone strong who will accept her for what she is. Can you do that?"

"That's the question, isn't it," Jake answered.

And here he was now, sitting next to Tanya asking himself that same question. If he were to stay, would he, could he, get close to someone like Tanya? It went against everything so far in his cold, hard life. Sure, he had moments of sentimentality, like when he had saved Jackie from her vicious pimp. But all and all he had been a pretty cold fish. He couldn't remember the last time he had anything that could be called a relationship. But what was he thinking? There was zero chance of him staying in Kalikastan.

Down in the paddock area, Chocolate was getting ready to run her first race of the day. She was as nervous as a kitten. Her diver had taken her out on a warm up lap. At first, she had been hesitant to put all of her weight on her injured leg, but a few cracks of the whip and a solid yank at her reins convinced her otherwise. Her breasts still stung from the beating that the female doctor had given her. She hadn't expected such cruelty from the gentle, seemingly loving woman. It pained her to think it, but it was just what she needed. It brought her right back to why she was here and what she had to do. Afterwards, the doctor had caressed her head and stroked her breasts until she calmed.

The lights went on on the tote board signifying that Chocolate's race was about to begin. Giorgi urged her up to the start line. He had watched the doctor slice the whip into the pony's breasts. It was the first thing that she had done that he totally agreed with aside from icing up Chocolate's leg. The doctor was attractive. He wondered if she had ever made it with a dwarf.

Fortunately, since Chocolate was right footed, the injury was to her left leg. The pony placed her right leg forward and dug it into the dirt of the track, she would use it for the all important push off. The track was still soft from the morning's grooming by the groundskeepers. Later, especially after the landaus had run, it would be packed and rutted. To have the track soft was an advantage for the slower ponies with greater endurance. The faster ones couldn't press them early on and develop a big lead. But in the afternoon, when the track was harder, the race would almost certainly go to the swift.

Chocolate was up against the seventh seed pony. The other pony, a pale skinned, red haired, Dutch female named Beatrice, in honor of their queen, wearing a purple and red hood, would run fast at the beginning of the race, trying to aggravate Chocolate's injury. There would be no chivalry today. Beatrice, unlike Felisa last night, faced elimination. She had lost to the number three pony yesterday, but had risen above her ranking to survive races with the fourth and fifth seeds.

The two ponies stood nervously, their right legs before them, waiting, but not for the sound of the gun. That was for the benefit of their drivers. They were waiting for their drivers' signals to begin. If the gun had gone and off and their drivers' did not react, they would have stayed just where they were. It was a pretty standard training technique, while practicing starts, to do nothing once every while after the starting gun sounded. The ponies who took a single step forward were beaten severely.

They might have saved all of their worrying. Although Beatrice did start out strong, the soft track was in Chocolate's favor for once. She stayed within striking range of the red tailed, Dutch pony and then, after the ¾ pole, overtook her with ease.

Watching the big breasted, purple and red hooded pony be driven back to her encampment, Jake felt sorry for her, knowing that her strenuous and heroic efforts to beat one of the best ponygirls around would be rewarded by having her beautiful, sweaty, pale skin adorned with long, angry, painful streaks of red.

Tanya's mother's race was at 11 and Lightning's next race was a short while after that. Jake readily agreed to Tanya's lewd suggestion that they go back to his caravan to fuck. Irkut gave him a merry wink as he and the young woman downed their drinks and left the grandstands. They made their way there holding hands, a rare concession to affection by the American fixer. When they arrived, they saw that Betty had been remounted at her stake outside and was kneeling in the grass, her oral services proffered to one and all passers by. Tanya gave a little grunt of disgust.

"What kind of man is this Mr. Burnham?" she asked Jake.

"Well, he's a vindictive son of a bitch, I can tell you that," Jake replied.

Tanya insisted on comforting the forlorn bird woman. Using a rag and a bucket she found nearby, she opened the little plastic beak that Betty wore and washed her chin and chest free of the leavings of her many customers. There was a watering can nearby and she gave the slave girl a long, refreshing drink. If Betty's collar had not been padlocked to the pole, Tanya would have released her.

Betty looked up at Jake dejectedly while Tanya cleaned her up. "There's nothing I can do," Jake answered her mentally.

As Tanya finished up with Betty, the bird woman tearfully murmured her thanks to the girl through her ring gagged mouth,

When the romantic couple entered the caravan, Jake noted that Orchid was not in her cage. In the middle cage was the other slave girl they had brought with them in the trailer, a tall, thin French girl with long, black hair and unhappy eyes. Her name was Giselle. She was one of the first graduates of Burnham's slave training facility and had become his most recent favorite before Orchid. She was lithe, with small, pointed breasts that sat high on her chest. Her lips and nose were thin and her arms and legs were long. Her head was covered with little black ringlets. She wore a gag and had her hands bound behind her. Tanya cooed as she examined her from outside her cage. "Let's play with her," she said to Jake. It was exactly what Jake had been thinking.

He released the nervous looking, pretty, slave girl from her cage and the three of them went into Jake's bedroom. Tanya stripped down immediately and then pushed the slave girl on the bed. While Jake watched, she released her hands from behind her back and tied them off to the headboard. Tanya them removed the girl's shield gag from her mouth.

"Oh, she's so pretty," Tanya said. Jake had disrobed and was sitting on the edge of the bed. The svelte Russian girl was lying next to the black haired female. She ran her hands over her firm breasts, cupping them, toying with them and pinching lightly the dark red nipples. Giselle's hips shifted slightly. Her look of apprehension had started to turn to one of lust. Tanya leaned over her and pressed their bare breasts together. She had her hands on either side of the girl's long, delicate face. She whispered to her something in Russian and took possession of her lips. Jake watched as the two female bodies began to writhe against one another. He stroked Tanya's smooth, pale back and ran his hands over her firm rear mounds. His cock was getting harder by the second.

Tanya moaned with pleasure and then slid her body off of the young girl's. Giselle's eyes were misty and her lips were parted and wet. Tanya turned to Jake. "Kiss her, Jake, while I kiss her tits."

Jake needed no more authorization than that. He leaned over the girl and, placing his hand on the side of her head, brought his lips to bear. She parted hers, her pink tongue wiping her lower lip in anticipation. Jake kissed her and the warmth of her mouth brought a tingle to his cock. Her tongue twisted and turned in a passionate dance with his. The girl's body stiffened and she gave out a deep sigh as Tanya began to suck on her stiff, left nipple while caressing and teasing the other breast with her hand.

Giselle, trained to be a responsive whore, pulled at the chains that bound her hands to the bed above her. Tanya had shifted nipples and the slave girl's chest rose and her back arched as she received the pleasurable sensations. Jake abandoned their kiss so that he could watch his lover in action. Her hand had slipped down Giselle's torso and had slid across the tattoo of the black headed, angry mastiff that she wore there, a stark contrast to her pale skin. Her legs had spread wide and her hips rose to welcome Tanya's playful hand as it captured her graceful love lips. Giselle's pussy was not bare as were those of most of the slave girls.

She wore a thin border of black pubic hair around her sex topped by a small beard that decorated her lower belly.

Tanya's pussy was also trimmed, not shaved. It was an enticing change from the ever visible, clean shaven quims that the slave girls carried with them between their legs. Jake had a hard time deciding which he liked best. The clear availability of a shaven pudendum was erotic and enticing. But the presence of pubic growth around a pussy was like a reference to the base and animalistic aspects of sex. Betty was a good example of that. The presence of her wild, mature patch below her strangely painted body made her seem exotic, especially when offset by her pale, white thighs. Variety, which was the spice of life, abounded in Kalikastan. How he would miss it.

Tanya's long, thin fingers dabbled amidst Giselle's thighs, dragging along the short, black pubic hairs and dribbling down the divide between her love lips. Jake could see evidence of the slave girl's nascent pleasure there glistening as Tanya eased the folds of her labia back.

"What a lovely pussy you have," Tanya whispered lustfully to the girl. She rose her body up and retook possession of the girl's lips while her hand delved inside her slit. Giselle moaned and gave a little whimper of lust as the two women kissed.

When Tanya rose from their kiss, she took hold of Jake's rampant cock. "Step between the slut's thighs," she ordered him hoarsely, her breath ragged with passion.

As Jake moved to accommodate his lover's desire, Tanya shifted herself until her pussy was poised above the slave girl's lips. She had placed her knees on either side of the girl's head. She leaned over and, upside down, gave the girl a passionate open mouthed kiss. "Suck on my pussy, slave girl, but don't make me come until I'm ready," she told her.

Jake's lover lowered her excited divide over the girl's face. Leaning forward, she took hold of Jake's cock and proffered it to her own lips. "Mmmmmmmmm...," she said, smiling at Jake. Jake moaned as the young woman absorbed his length into her mouth until his cock rubbed against the back of her throat.

The Russian girl had taken possession of both him and the French slave girl. She was master of ceremonies as she enjoyed pleasure at both ends. Her free hand continued to worry the slave girl's slit and even as Jake groaned with pleasure, he could hear the slave girl's pants and moans of lust as she serviced her mistress.

Twice, while they frantically copulated, Jake heard the slave girl come. Giselle's thighs were divided by his legs as he stood between them and, when her orgasms overtook her, she tried in vain to bring them together to assuage the tormenting effects of Tanya's caresses. She must have paused in her administration of her tongue and lips to Tanya's twat as her body shook beneath her for, during one of her lustful explosions, Tanya broke her oral attentions to Jake's cock and commanded her to "Keep sucking, slut! Lick my cunt!" She gave the girl's pudenda two sharp slaps that made her jump and squeal. When the girl resumed her duties, Tanya recommenced her manual pleasuring of the girl's slit and took possession once more of Jake's stiff, thick cock with her lips.

Jake's cock welcomed the Russian girl's expert attentions to it. Her tongue ran around its fat head and she hummed and moaned as she serviced him, transferring the vibrations of her throat to his prick. Jake pumped his hips back at the mouth that was so passionately driving his lusts.

He wanted to come but dared not disappoint his lover. He wanted to wait until she did and was struggling to hold back until her command.

Suddenly, Tanya released Jake's cock from her lips and leaned back. She grabbed the slave girl's thighs and drew them back, making her slit rise up and beg for Jake's attention. "Fuck her, Jake! Tanya shouted. "Put your cock in her!"

Jake obeyed without hesitation. The black shrouded orifice split easily as his prick drove between her engorged love lips. Tanya was riding the girl's face, moaning. Her breasts jumped up and down enticingly. She reached out her hand and took possession of Jake's face, bringing it towards hers. Their lips married and Jake felt his dam about to burst. "Now! Now!" he thought madly. "Come now!"

Tanya, as if she had read his mind, called out to the slave girl, "Make me come! Suck my clit! Harder! Harder!" As her right hand caressed her lover's face, her left was frantically stroking the slave girl's pleasure bud.

Jake held on for dear life. The slave girl's legs were over his shoulders. When Tanya's body started to quake and shudder, when she moaned and gripped his face with all her might, when her tongue thrust itself deeply into his mouth, Jake came. His cock burst into a series of sharp eruptions. Giselle, whose plush crevasse he was still plowing heartily, issued a muffled groan of her own and her pussy began to contract and pulse around his meat. They had all come at once! Jake was delirious. He had had threesomes before, but Tanya had put together a masterpiece. He came and came and came.

All three of the lovers collapsed at the same time. Tanya slipped off the girl's face and pulled Jake forwards until his slippery, soft, but still engorged cock slid from the slave girl's crevasse. Their bodies intertwined atop her soft, lithe flesh.

They lay there catching their collective breaths. After a while, Tanya pushed Jake aside and gave the panting Giselle a soulful kiss. "What a good little slave girl you are," she said affectionately and kissed her again. The slave girl gave a tentative smile. She was not used to such effusion from anyone who took pleasure from her body in Kalikastan. Tanya's emissions were smeared across her face. Tanya wiped them clear with her hand. "Kiss her Jake, tell her how good she was."

Jake was slightly offput by Tanya's instructions, but leaned over and gave her a kiss anyway. "You're a good slut," he said.

Tanya laughed. "Well put, Jake!" she said. "Well put!"

The Russian girl explored the slave girl's body with her hand. "You're so smooth and pretty," she told her. "Do you think you can get my fiancé's cock hard again?"

The girl looked uneasily at Jake. "Yes, Mistress," she said tentatively.

Tanya unlocked the girl's hands from over her head. "Lie down, Jake," she told him. "Let the slave girl suck your prick."

Jake's piece gave a little twitch at the thought of the beautiful, black haired girl's lips around it. His hand was stroking her thin, well toned thigh. "You're awfully free with my cock," he told Tanya, laughing.

He lay down and the slave girl set herself between his knees. She cupped her hands around his balls and started a gentle nibbling at the beefy head of his manhood. Tanya lay by his side, her hand lazily running across his chest, nuzzled in the crux of his arm. Jake lay mesmerized by the soft lips that teased his cock and the warmth of his lover's body next to him.

As his cock began to fill with blood once again, Tanya rose up on her elbow and presented her lips to his. They engaged in a desultory, mellow kiss. It was pleasant to be worked on by two pairs of luxurious lips at once, receiving pleasure high and low. The slave girl was caressing his thighs while she suckled at his meat. His lust was growing. When his cock stood up rigid and firm, Giselle looked up at Tanya with a proud look on her face.

It was amazing to Jake how these Russian women got the slave girls to worship them. Ilona had had the same look this morning when Dr. Kevsky let her suckle on her breast. A little kindness seemed to go a long way, but it was more than that. The Russian women seemed to have the power to enthrall the slave girls, regardless of the fact that they held them cruelly in bondage. Svetlana had whipped Ilona's breasts, yet the girl seemed to adore her. Tanya had given the French slut two hard cracks on her puss a little while ago, but the slave girl seemed to have accepted that as Tanya's right.

The blond Russian girl smiled at the slave girl. "Good work, Giselle," she said. "Keep on going, but don't let him come."

Tanya rose and slid behind the black haired slave. She pressed her body up against her while her hands circled around her torso and took hold of her pointy breasts. Jake watched as Tanya massaged them, stroking down their conical surfaces and then teasing the tips with her forefingers and thumbs. The slave girl gave out a little moan. Jake watched, his cock loving Giselle's slow, tantalizing pleasuring of it, while Tanya moved to the girl's side and slipped her hand under her between her thighs.

She started to caress her there with one hand while the other continued to worry and massage her breasts.

"I want you to come, little slave girl," she told her. "Come with my lover's cock in your mouth." Giselle shuddered at her mistress's invitation. She moaned as her pussy was worked by Tanya's magic hand. Jake felt her moans on his cock and a shiver went up his body. When Giselle came, her lips pulsed on his cock in sympathy with her throbbing cleft. She was so overwhelmed with pleasure that she had to halt her ministrations to Jake's manhood in order to endure it.

Tanya made the girl come twice and then urged her off of Jake's rigid rod. "Let me finish him off," she said. "Go give him your lips."

Giselle made room for Tanya at Jake's loins. Jake groaned when Tanya's mouth encircled him. Her tongue washed his shaft energetically. Her lips gripped him firmly as she slid them up and down. Her hand had his tender stones in its grip and she was fondling it while her other hand stroked his belly.

The slave girl approached Jake tentatively, almost shyly. She gave him a smile and put her lips on his. Their roles now reversed, the two women brought their skills to bear on his body. Giselle's hand lightly stroked his chest while Tanya's caressed her belly. He felt his crisis coming and he groaned deeply into the slave girl's mouth. "Mmmmmmmmmmmm!" he moaned as his cock started to twitch. "Mmmmmmmmm! Mmmmmmmmmm!" His manhood pulsed in the hot mouth of his lover. Tanya energetically encouraged the throbbing pole with her tongue and lips. As his forces ebbed, she playfully took the knob between her lips and gave him one more hearty suck.

"Ohhhhhhhh," Jake moaned. He was as limp as wet toast. Tanya came and snuggled next to him opposite Giselle.

"That's how it will be when we're married, Jake," she said. Jake was too relaxed to argue with her. What was the sense when he would be gone in two days? But the thought of many hours of explosive sex with Tanya directing the slave girls on how to best pleasure his body was a tempting thought.

Tanya looked at the clock on the wall. "We've got to get going or we'll miss my mother's race," she told Jake. Getting up was the last thing that Jake wanted to do, but he dragged himself to full consciousness and began to dress. Tanya, too, threw her clothes on. She was wearing her standard jeans and t-shirt, a combination that seemed to suit her well. After they dressed, Tanya fastened the slave girls hands back behind her. She then took the long, thick, leather gag and pushed it in between Giselle's sad lips. The lustful Russian girl passed her hand through the slave girl's short, black ringlets. "Maybe we'll see each other again, Giselle," she said. "Would you like that?"

The melancholy slave girl gave a silent nod of her head. Tanya kissed her small, pointed breasts and led her back to her cage.

Irkut was waiting for them when they returned to the grandstands. They ordered up some hot food from a slave girl and some drinks.

The food and beverage service in the box seats was done on a kind of honor system. No slave girl had the right to refuse an order, but it was understood that the patrons would not interfere with their duties. And it was considered rather poor manners to cheat one of them by not paying even though they were hardly in a position to demand it.

As far as sexual services were concerned, you could purchase a token at a booth near the admissions gate and exchange it for oral delight from any of the slave girls marked for service. They typically wore a red tag affixed to their collars so that you could tell them from the slave girls who were performing specific duties for their masters. Not that the other slave girls could refuse an order to get to their knees, but heaven help you if their masters learned why they were late and the otherwise docile creature pointed you out.

As far as the hoi polloi was concerned, down in the reserved seats or with standing room only, there was a brothel tent behind the huge grandstand structure and food was all self service from booths. Some of the great unwashed brought slave girls that they had purchased on the second or third hand markets, but for many Kalikastani's, owning their own slave girl was more of an ambition than a reality. Mostly, the general public left their slave girls back at their campsites bound and gagged. There were special belts that locked into place so that no one would use them without permission. Once in a while, you heard of someone actually stealing a slave girl, but that was rare and very harshly punished.

Irkut was dutifully reading the racing form to determine his next bet. The race was between two sets of yearlings pulling two pony carts. To Jake, they looked skittish and nervous as they ran their warm up lap. During the tournament, except for the championship races, only one warm up lap was allowed. It was up to the drivers and his grooms to massage and loosen the ponies' leg and shoulder muscles before they got to the start up line.

While the yearlings slowly approached the start line, four shapely, young, hooded ponies with long, bare legs and naked, swaying breasts, Jake drifted his binoculars across the track and over to the paddock area. "Look," he told Tanya, "there's your mother." Helena and her other two daughters were busy warming her delectable, Irish ponies up. Lada, the wraithlike, younger sister, had her hand between one of the ponies' thighs, stoking her lusts before the big event. Jake thought it was Claire, if he remembered their order correctly. They looked so much the same. Zoya, the brazen, older one, was stroking another's thighs with both her hands, getting the blood to flow there freely. Helena was walking back and forth double and triple checking the ponies' rigging.

Tanya took the glasses from Jake and looked for herself. "Oh, I hope she does well," she said. "She's running against the first seed. I know she won't win, but I really want her to give the other team a good race."

Jake turned back to the track. The four yearlings were lined up at the start. Knowing that these ponies were probably no more than three or four months old, as age in ponygirl racing was measured, that is, by the time since they had been dehumanized, he figured that memories of their prior lives must still be fresh in their minds. What a shock it must be to see the kind of crowds that gathered to witness their degraded state and their use as beasts of burden. He wondered why they didn't just collapse to their knees and cry, overwhelmed by what they had become. But, then again, he had never lived a life under the whip, ruled by conscienceless men whose strength and will geometrically outweighed his.

The yearling races were fun to watch. The ponies, well trained runners by this point in the season, were sprightly and eager. The one set had dark tan skin and black ponytails, either Italian or Greek, Jake speculated. The other yearlings were pale skinned with blond hair. They could have been from almost anywhere. When Jake asked Irkut to check the program, it turned out that the dark pony was actually Honduran, a first for the tournament. The blonds were a combination of a young American pony and a Dane. Jake wondered if the American pony had traveled to Kalikastan on Air Burnham.

It turned out to be a good race. The lead exchanged several times and it was a close finish. What more could you ask for? Irkut had picked the winner.

When Helena's team came to the line to run, Tanya could barely contain her excitement. The two six pony teams jumped off at the start, but you could have gone home right there. The other team had been, according to Irkut, running together for three years. You could tell from their incredible precision how well trained they were. They took the turns smooth as silk and there were no wasted movements. Although Helena's team made a good run for it at the end, coming within two lengths, her defeat and exit from the tournament was decisive.

Tanya was in tears. Jake held her close and tried to comfort her. "She did well for the first time in the tournament, Tanya," he tried to tell her, but she just cried and cried. Surreptitiously, Irkut showed Jake his ducat. He had bet on the winner.

When Tanya finally stopped crying, she apologized and said that she had to go and be with her mother. Jake told her that he understood, but that he had to stay and see what happened with Chocolate.

"Please come tonight, Jake," she begged. "It would mean a lot to my mother and to me."

"I promise," he answered. Wiping her eyes with her t-shirt, Tanya smiled and left.

CHAPTER SIX

Anton Drabik had watched Chocolate's victory with philosophical resignation. She had one more race to run and she would probably qualify for the finals tomorrow, depending on the outcome of the other races. Lightning had already won her first heat today and it was likely that after the next two, one against a very low seed which had overachieved so far in the tournament, she would be in the championship final for her division as well. Burnham and Grobgy had finalized the plans for the match race the day after and met with racing officials to sign a formal agreement and to work out the details of the contest.

It was hoped by the racing officials that many people would stay the extra day, generating additional revenues in camping fees, food sales and other amenities. The side show vendors had been encouraged to remain until the match was over and most had agreed. A fireworks display and live music, paid for by the American, Michael Burnham, had been arranged for the night between the finals and the match race so that people would be entertained. The challenge race between Chocolate and Lightning would be good for business, good for the sport, good for everybody, except Anton Drabik.

He had had enough of sitting in the owner's booth. The presence of Grobgy, the bastard who had agreed to put Lightning at risk, and his devil daughter Anya was too much to take. He sat in one of the box seats that Grobgy had bought for his staff, some of whom were accomplices in his bid to overthrow the former N.K.V.D. sergeant. It was important for Drabik to maintain contact with them and keep them happy. He had purchased a few slave girls over at the second hand booths for them to play with over the tournament. This morning, after finally releasing the big breasted, blond slave girl he had been abusing, he purchased one for himself.

The girl had long, auburn hair and grapefruit sized breasts. She was not thin, he really didn't like them that way, but she was not zaftig either. The sales tent had been overstocked and he was able to make a good deal. He had brought her back to his tent for the obligatory whipping that a master always gave a new slave girl. When he had fucked her, she was very enthusiastic, eager to please her new owner.

Her name was Antonia and she was an Italian slut. Drabik had had enough of the American wenches. Every time he fucked one he thought of Lightning, or as he now knew, Maddy. Her face from the picture he had of her before her kidnapping haunted him. He had burned the original, both for security reasons and to try and block the reminder of her humanity from his mind. He was successful in the former, so far, in that as far as he could tell, no one knew that he had discovered her identity and her connection to the American billionaire, but had been unsuccessful as to the second. Every time that he saw Lightning taken out on the track for one of her heats, his stomach tightened and his heart rate went up. Desire was a terrible thing when frustrated.

He watched Lightning cruise through her next heat, his new slave girl kneeling beside him gagged and bound and connected to his chair by a leash.

Antonia had led a rather sheltered life as a slave girl. After her training, she had been delivered to a mid level bureaucrat in the Kalikastani government. Even though the country was a quasi nation run by gangsters, there were still some governmental functions that needed to be performed. Taxes needed to be collected, laws, such as they were, administered. There was a rudimentary, if unreliable, court system.

Antonia's owner worked in the Health Ministry and oversaw regulation of the nation's hospitals. He went to work regularly like a real bureaucrat and came home every day at the same time. He was a widower and lived with his 22 year old daughter and a native Kalikastani housekeeper. Antonia had been a gift to him from his coworkers when his wife died, something that he had appreciated as being very thoughtful.

The man had few sexual idiosyncrasies. He never whipped the girl; she always seemed properly compliant and obedient. When her master was not home, Antonia was charged with assisting the housekeeper in her duties, cleaning, doing the washing, things like that.

The daughter, Rowena, a shy, rather plain, blonde girl who attended the University in Dlitski, the capital, at first resented the presence of the beautiful, always naked, dark skinned slave girl. She was embarrassed and repelled when, each night when her father came home, he took the pretty slave into his bedroom for a relaxing blow job before dinner. She heard them coupling in the bedroom next to hers almost every night. The girl's beauty was a constant reproach to her. She insisted that the creature be kept caged in her father's bedroom when she was not performing her duties around the house.

The presence of the slave became virtually intolerable for her when one day when she had come home unexpectedly early from class. She had been confronted by a disgusting scene. The housekeeper, a sixtyish, dark skinned, heavy set, peasant woman was sitting on the edge of a straight backed chair in the middle of their parlor with her skirts up around her waist. Antonia was kneeling before her, her arms bound behind her back, and was giving the woman oral service. The housekeeper, embarrassed, jumped up and quickly hustled the slave girl into the master bedroom. It was something that the women never spoke about afterwards.

One day, though, Rowena came home to they house in a terribly depressed mood. She had been seeing this boy, her first real romantic entanglement, and the boy had told her that day after school that he was breaking up with her. He had started seeing one of the more attractive girls in their class.

Rowena was heartbroken. The housekeeper was apparently out doing some shopping and had left Antonia kneeling chained to the balustrade of the stairs that led to the upper floors of the house. She was gagged and had her hands bound behind her as befitted proper slave protocol.

The distraught girl threw herself on the couch in the parlor and began to cry her eyes out. She had held it in all the way home and when she crossed the threshold of the house, the dam burst. She sobbed for several long minutes. When she began to recover, she saw the attractive, lithe slave girl looking at her. In Rowena's mind the slave girl was mocking her. In actuality, Antonia felt sorry for the somewhat chunky, plain girl. It was the first real sign of emotion she had seen in a very long time. Rowena, misreading the slave girl's doleful look, jumped up and grabbed the thin cane from the umbrella stand that the housekeeper used occasionally, but very rarely, to discipline the slave. She raised it over her head and struck Antonia six or seven times with all of her might.

"How dare you look at me, you whore!" she screamed. "I'll whip you until you bleed!" Antonia cringed as the cane viciously struck her arms, her back and her thighs. She prayed that this was not some new development in her life as an embonded servant, and it hurt her terribly that the young girl would treat her so shabbily.

When Rowena paused in her assault to catch her breath, she saw the tears flowing from the slave girl's eyes. The realization that she had committed an abuse against the flesh of the defenseless, young woman horrified her. She threw the cane aside and knelt down on the floor and began to hug the piteous slave girl. "Oh, I'm sorry! I'm sorry!" she cried. She hugged the shapely, soft body of the slavegirl tightly. Antonia, whose eyes had been tearing anyway, broke into heartfelt sobs. No one had treated her with compassion since the day of her kidnapping many months ago.

A native of Genoa, and a little over 20 years old, she had been visiting the small, seaside town of San Lucido in the province of Calabria with her boyfriend. It was a beautiful, early summer vacation, when the beaches of that small tourist town were not as scorching as they would become in July and August. She had been attending the University studying Italian history and she was anxious to see some of the ancient Greek temples and ruins further on to the south.

That night, they had dinner in a small taverna near the waterfront specializing in the fruits of Mare Nostrum, as the Italians call the great sea that surrounds their peninsular nation. Alberto had gotten quite drunk on the local wine and became involved in a hot discussion on Italian politics with some of the other patrons. Antonia had asked him several times to come back with her to the hotel. This was not turning out to be the romantic evening she had anticipated. Finally, frustrated by Alberto's refusal to leave, she had walked out of the restaurant alone to head back to their hotel.

It was a pleasant evening, a little after midnight, and the streets were mostly deserted. The hotel was about ten blocks from the restaurant. When she had walked about three blocks, a car came by along the esplanade. It slowed down as it passed her and then speeded back up. Antonia could see that there were three men in it.

Now, Italy remains one of the bastions of male chauvinism in Europe, especially in the south. There was nothing unusual in men slowing down to gawk at a solitary young woman walking along late at night. Antonia was shapely and she was wearing a tight, bright red, tube top and a knee length denim skirt that hugged her delectable hips snugly.

The car, a late model, black, Fiat coupe, rounded the corner about three blocks up and sped away. A few minutes later, it came around behind her once again. This time, Antonia could see the men peering out at her and smiling lasciviously. The car stopped about two blocks ahead of her and one of the men got out. It then turned the corner once more.

The pretty girl was nervous at the presence of the man ahead of her, but she kept walking, keeping her head down, determined not to be intimidated by the men's little games.

When the car came around the third time, she knew something was up. It came to a sudden stop right next to her and another of the men hopped out. She tried to make a run for it, but the high heeled sandals she was wearing impeded her. She realized immediately that she was caught between the man in front of her and the man behind. To her right were some closed up shops and to her left, the sandy beaches of the Mediterranean.

Realizing that she would not make it to the hotel, which was still three blocks away, she made a dash for the beach, hoping to outflank the man ahead of her. She made it over the small boardwalk and onto the sand. Hopping on the soft, sandy surface, she removed one sandal and then the other so that she could run faster. She often, later, tried to explain to herself why she had not cried out. Maybe it was because her throat was dry with fear; maybe it was because she was having a hard time believing that what was happening was really happening. Maybe it was because she had always thought of herself as an independent, self reliant young woman, or maybe it was just panic.

In any case, she did not cry out or scream. After she had pulled off her sandals, she made it three more steps when the man who had been in front of her tackled her. They rolled around on the sand for a few moments until the man from behind caught up. The first man had his hand over her mouth and she bit into it fiercely. He yelled in pain. Now she was ready to scream for help, but it was too late. The second man leapt onto her and pushed her face into the sand. While her long, smooth, graceful legs, kicked and jerked in an attempt to free her, strong hands brought her arms together and tied them off with some kind of belt.

Her mouth was full of sand when she was able to raise up her head and she began to spit it out prefatory to a loud call for help. A cloth was pressed against her face and shoved between her outstretched lips. She was flipped over and a fist smashed into her belly, knocking all of the air out of her. Quickly, before she could recover, the men dragged her across the sand to the street where the car was waiting. She was shoved into the back seat. She heard the doors to the car slam and a hood was pulled over her head. Her body was shoved down onto the floor and heavy boots pressed down on her. Within a few moments, the car was speeding along the beachfront street. It made a turn and, after negotiating the narrow streets of the town, hit the main road and headed into the hills overlooking the city.

She was held in a little farmhouse for two days, naked and chained to a bed, blindfolded. The men used her repeatedly and the man she had bitten whipped her severely with his belt. She never saw the men's faces except for the brief glances she had gotten when she was struggling with them during her capture. Three more girls were collected and late one night they were all loaded into the back of a van and taken down to the docks of a village further north.

Hooded, bound and gagged, naked as she had been kept since her kidnapping, she was loaded along with the other girls onto a fishing boat and taken to Sicily. Her accommodations there were a bit more formal, as she was held in a cage amidst a series of fifteen or so in the cellar of some old fortress. Since sunlight never reached her little prison and she spent most of her time blindfolded anyway, she was not sure how long she was kept there. After what she thought was four or maybe five days, she and the other girls, their numbers had grown to twelve, were loaded onto the back of a truck late at night. They were taken inland about 40 or so miles, by her estimation. There, in a long field that once served as an impromptu Word War Two aerodrome, the girls were loaded onto a plane and flown away.

Since then, she had heard virtually nary a kind word. It goes without saying that she suffered a harsh period of slave training during which her name was tattooed on her chest and the snarling head of a tiger was etched into her lower belly. She learned her slave lessons well, having given up all hope of a return to sunny Italy anytime soon. When she was bought, she had the usual fears and trepidations of a new slave girl as to what her fate might be.

Being settled into the two story house near the center of the city as a concubine to the middle aged, unimaginative man had been a blessing. His use of her was perfunctory and the old housekeeper was not cruel to her, although she treated her as the slave that she was. The old lady kept her clean, fed her, shaved her sex every day and even took her on walks through the city on a leash connected to her slave collar, her mouth gagged and her arms bound behind her, so that she could get some exercise.

It was, at first, hard to get used to parading through the residential streets of the seemingly modern city leashed like a pet, naked as the day she was born but for her slave regalia. She blushed when the men and women, even youngsters, ogled her ample, bare breasts or the clean shaven surface of her pudenda. She got used to it though very quickly as she often saw other slave girls, similarly bereft of any modest coverings, being led about as she was. Sometimes the old lady stopped to talk with one of the neighboring housekeepers on a similar mission and Antonia would look knowingly and with commiseration into the eyes of the slave girl on the end of the other woman's leash. When Antonia saw the bruises and welts that the other girls often wore, she understood how lucky she had it.

But her heart had been closed in that little farmhouse in Calabria as the men pierced her defenseless love lips with their pricks, or forced them between her sullen lips. She spoke only a little English and virtually no Russian beyond 'nyet' and 'da'. The old lady tried to teach her some, but in the seven months she had been there, Antonia had learned very little. The old lady was usually nice, but not what you would call kind. The young girl had been aloof from her and Antonia had felt her animosity often when she knelt in the parlor, hands bound behind her and wearing her gag, while they watched television or listened to the radio. She blanched each time when, in front of the girl, the man took hold of the ring in the front of her slave collar and escorted her to his bedroom for a fuck or a blowjob. At night, in spite of the man's lack of imagination in the bedroom and quickly satisfied lust, she did call out in pleasure sometimes, and she knew that the girl almost certainly heard her outbursts of passion.

To feel the girl's arms around her in an earnest expression of remorse and sympathy was too much for Antonia to take. Slave girls need to be tough, theirs is a forlorn lot. But even they are human and can only take so much. All of her sorrow of the past eight months came bursting out. She cried and cried and cried.

Rowena did not know what to do. She had not intended to cause the unfortunate girl such misery. She and some of her friends at the university often spoke, in low tones of course, of the terrible institution of female slavery, although that sentiment did not always extend to ponygirls and was mostly proffered by female rather than male students. A couple of her friends had made up a leaflet denouncing the evil institution and passed it out one day in the University commons. They were arrested, of course, and had not been heard from since.

Frantic to stop the girl's manic sobs, Rowena removed her gag and began to stroke her head and kiss her on the lips. Suddenly, the heat of the girl's naked body exuded through her plain white, cotton blouse and her thin, cotton skirt. Rowena felt something move inside her. Her hand was on the slave girl's arm and she slid it subtly to the girl's bare breast. She held the round, firm orb lightly, appreciating its mass and its softness. Gently closing her hand around the hot mammary, Rowena let her lips fall on the girl's dark, smooth, soft neck. Her other hand was behind the slave girl's back and she pulled her towards her.

Antonia had stopped crying. The warmth of the girl's hand, her tender touch, her soft lips on her neck sent a shiver of passion through her. She did not want to make an untoward advance to her in fear that she would frighten the blond haired girl and she would stop. Her hands were bound together by the wrists behind her anyway. The girl's lips rose over Antonia's chin, across her cheek and found her mouth. Antonia parted her lips and let the girl's hungry tongue inside.

The two young women, one free and one slave, kissed each other passionately. Rowena's hand drifted over the slave girl's taut belly and then stroked her long, tender thigh. She was afraid to center her hand on the slave's smooth, hairless sex, not sure if she wanted to give in to the lustful urges she was having. Antonia pressed her body against the young girl's and moaned.

Just then, the two women heard the sounds of someone coming up the steps outside. A key entered the lock to the outer door. Rowena quickly broke their embrace and picked up the gag she had removed a short while before. She gave the slave girl a quick peck on the cheek and reinstalled it. She had just gotten the thing buckled back behind her head when the door opened. It was separated from the rest of the house by a small vestibule and Rowena had just enough time to dash across the parlor and take a sitting position on one of the soft, overstuffed chairs.

When she entered the house, the housekeeper sensed that something was not as it should be. She looked at the slave girl and noticed that her eyes were soft and unfocused. She looked across the parlor and saw Rowena sitting there trying to look innocent, reading a magazine that had been on the coffee table. Her face was flushed and she was panting.

Unfortunately for Rowena and Antonia, the cane that had been used as the catalyst for their two minutes of lust was lying on the floor not far from the olive skinned slave girl. She also had several angry, red marks across her arms and legs. Greta, that was the housekeeper's name, at first did not know what to make of it. Clearly, Rowena had beaten the slave girl, but she was sure that something more had happened.

Greta had been a young girl once too. While a teenager, she had worked for one of the Communist Party leaders as a maid. The Revolution was supposed to have done away with such menial jobs, but the Revolution had stultified many years before. Female slavery had never really gone away in the Kalikastani Soviet Socialist Republic, it was just better hidden and not as blatant as it was today. The Commissar held in thrall a beautiful, pale skinned young girl, the daughter of some convicted 'counterrevolutionaries'. One day, she had found the girl naked and crying in the Commissar's bedroom, chained to the bed. She had comforted the pretty girl and one thing had led to another. Their affair had lasted several years right under the nose of the Commissar until, one day, the Commissar was purged and shot. The young girl was sent off to a labor camp and Greta never saw her again.

The wily housekeeper realized exactly what had happened. She had been living in fear that Rowena would tell her father about what she had seen that day when she came home early. This was the opportunity to make sure she kept quiet about it.

"What's going on?" she said innocently, putting down her shopping bag and picking up the cane. "Did you whip Antonia?"

Rowena knew that she could not talk away the bruises on the slave girl or the cane on the floor. "Y-yes," she said tentatively, thinking quickly. "She was looking at me rudely and refused to stop so I beat her."

"Ohhhhhh," Greta replied. "That's very bad. I'll have to give her a good licking after dinner. Maybe I should tell your father. He might want to beat her himself."

"Nooo!" Rowena exclaimed more excitedly than she intended. "That's all right. I corrected her and that should be that. She doesn't need to be beaten and I don't want Father to be bothered by what was really a trivial incident."

"But this is very serious, Rowena. I have been around slave girls most of my life and I know that if you let something like this slip by, who could tell what could happen next."

The blond haired girl was panicked. "Please, Greta, don't tell my father. It was only a little look and I may have overreacted. I was irritable and maybe I acted too quickly."

"Well," the old lady said returning the cane to its holder, "if that's the way it was, I won't tell your father. But she'll still need to be punished. I'll give her ten strokes after your father goes to bed."

Greta picked up the bag of groceries, unhooked Antonia from the balustrade and went into the kitchen to make dinner.

All evening long, Rowena fretted about the pain and torment that the slave girl was going to have to suffer because of her own stupidity. Antonia, although she had not fully understood the words that the housekeeper had said, had gotten the distinct impression that something was going to happen to her that was not pleasant.

When the father came home, Rowena had to run to her room and cry after she watched him take Antonia to his bedroom for some oral delight. At dinner, while Antonia knelt naked and bound near the corner of the table between Rowena and her father, she cast miserable glances at the slave girl. When they sat down in the living room and listened to a symphony on the radio, she bounced her legs nervously while on the edge of tears.

At about nine thirty, her father took Antonia off to the bedroom. He almost always went to bed early and was off to the Ministry at 7 A.M. Rowena tip toed past his bedroom door and heard him grunting and Antonia moaning. She ran off to her bedroom, threw herself down on her bed, and cried.

It was Greta's custom to retrieve Antonia from the father's bedroom when he was finished with her and give her her bath. It was one of Greta and Antonia's secrets that the old housekeeper often helped the young slave girl release her passion from what was usually an unsatisfying fuck with the old man. Greta had a little radio that she played in the bathroom to disguise Antonia's moans of pleasure. Rowena had heard the noises the slave girl made from time to time, but hadn't given them much thought.

When Rowena heard the bathtub running, her heart went out to the slave girl. It seemed that Greta was saving her beating for the last thing of the night so that she could appreciate it better as she tried to fall asleep in her little cage in Rowena's father's room.

The bath took a long time. Greta took special effort to make the slave girl smell and look pretty. She raised, but did not satisfy, the lustful girl's passions by stroking her soft, pleasant quim and sucking on her long, thick teats.

Rowena had been in hell waiting for the housekeeper and the slave girl to emerge from the bath. She had resolved to tell Greta everything and to beg her not to beat her. When the bathroom door cracked open, Rowena was right there.

"Oh, Greta, please don't beat Antonia, please! It was all my fault! I shouldn't have struck her; she didn't do anything wrong!" Rowena's imploring words were stated passionately but softly so as not to awaken her father.

Greta, holding the ring to Antonia's collar in her hand, stopped walking towards the stairs. "Then why did you strike her?" she asked.

"Because I was upset. My boyfriend broke up with me and I was angry and Antonia looked at me and I went wild," Rowena explained hurriedly, the words being emitted in a torrent.

"But that's not all that happened, is it Rowena? Tell me the truth!"

Tears flowing down her face, ashamed at having to confess her lesbian like act, Rowena whined, "I was so sorry that I hit her that I went to comfort her and then, and then,…"

"And then you kissed her. Is that what you're trying to tell me?"

"Yes, yes," Rowena cried back. "I didn't mean to but I was overwhelmed and she felt so good. I'll never do it again, I promise! Just don't beat her, please! It's all my fault!"

Rowena had fallen to her knees while pleading with the old woman. Greta took her free hand and caressed Greta's blond covered head. "It's all right, Rowena," she said. "It's all right. That's what Antonia is here for. She is a creature of delight and her flesh is almost irresistible. When I was a young girl, I fell in love with a slave girl too."

"Oh, thank you, Greta," Rowena said. "Thank you."

"And to show you that I understand, I'm going to let Antonia spend a little time with you in your room. It'll be our little secret, won't it?"

Rowena was ecstatic at the thought of putting her lips on Antonia's again. "Yes! Yes!" she said, nodding emphatically.

Greta urged Rowena up from the floor and presented the slave girl to her. "I'll give you two hours," she said. "Then I have to put Antonia to bed. Do you understand?"

"Yes! Yes!" Rowena said eagerly.

"And not a word to anyone," Greta said.

The delighted, impassioned young girl took hold of Antonia's collar and pulled her into her bedroom, shutting the door. The slave girl was wearing her shield gag that covered the lower portion of her face. Rowena tore it off and pulled their bodies together. Their kiss of earlier that day was duplicated a hundred fold. Rowena backed Antonia up against her bed until she fell down atop it. She climbed on top of her and mashed their bodies together. Her hands were all over the slave girl, her breasts, her thighs, her belly. She realized after a while that Antonia's hands were locked behind her back. She climbed off of the girl and pulled her up so that she could have access to her hands. When they were freed, the two desperately passionate young women threw their arms about each other and kissed fervently.

Slowly, but surely, Antonia's greater experience and deeper sensuality began to tell. The one who was the mistress became the slave and vice versa. Rowena was still dressed and Antonia slowly, leisurely, while kissing Rowena's face and neck unbuttoned her blouse, revealing her heavy, pale orbs. With one motion she used her hands to slide the blouse and the straps of her plain white brassiere off of her shoulders. She used her knowledgeable lips to caress Rowena's chest while she snuck her hands behind the girl and unsnapped her bra. Slowly, expertly, almost without the young girl realizing it, she lowered the blouse and bra off of her.

Rowena's pride was revealed. Her breasts were as pale as snow. Her teats and areola were almost pink. Here and there, the almost perfect white surface of her bosom was marred by the slight suggestion of a pale blue vein. Her nervousness was evidence that she was a real, unpretentious woman, revealing her secret charms to a lover for the first time.

Antonia kissed Rowena's stiff nipples and sucked on them until the young girl moaned. She caressed the heft of her prominent mounds. Antonia had learned well the Sapphic arts while in training as a slave girl and she was bringing all of her disused skills to bear on her mistress, enrapturing her, rewarding her for her kindness.

Rowena felt momentarily frightened when she felt Antonia's hand creep up under her pale, blue dress and onto her thigh. "This is really going to happen," she thought as she kissed her embonded lover. Her belly fluttered as the hand passed over the gusset of her panties and across her belly. Rowena was by no means a thin girl. She was ashamed of her heaviness and the fold of fat she saw on her stomach when she sat down on her bed nude. She was frightened that when Antonia saw it, she would laugh or feel repulsed by it.

Antonia was a skilled, conscientious lover. She felt the girl's fear and, after giving her mistress a passionate kiss, stood up from the bed and turned off the small table lamp that had lit their passions so far. The room was plunged into a semi-darkness lit only by the streetlamp outside Rowena's window. Careful not to beak the spell she had woven, Antonia loosened the waistband of Rowena's skirt and then dragged it and her white cotton panties over her hips and down her thighs. Gently and slowly, she lifted each of Rowena's legs until the garments were free of her body. Leaving her lover trembling in the darkness, Antonia turned and pulled down the covers to Rowena's bed. It was a single bed, appropriate for the prim daughter of a governmental bureaucrat. But there was room for both of them there. The slave girl urged Rowena forward until both of their bodies lay atop the cool, white sheets. She turned the blond woman to her back and climbed between her legs, letting the heat of her body enflame the young girl.

If you have ever made love to a slave girl and allowed her absolute freedom to ply her trade upon your flesh, then you know what Rowena experienced that night, made more precious and exciting because it was her first time. Antonia explored every inch of Rowena's body with her tongue and lips. She made the slightly plump girl moan and groan with desire and pleasure. Placing her face between the girl's outstretched thighs, she licked and kissed her engorged, virginal labia and then sucked hard on the small digit atop them.

The slave girl wanted to see the face of her lover when she came. It was the first time she had made love to anyone under her free will since she had been kidnapped eight or nine months ago. Her body had been violated by dozens of men since then, perhaps a hundred, she had lost count. Sometimes she had been hooded or blindfolded when she was raped during her training period and did not know if her assaults came from men who had already used her in one way or another or different, unknown men. They had taught her that the identity of her sexual partner was irrelevant to her duty to give him or her absolute delight, all of her passion, all of her lust. But tonight it did matter. Tonight she was making love with someone who had kissed her from compassion and deep affection. She did not know if she would get another chance and she wanted this time to count.

Once she knew that the Russian girl's lusts were prepared to boil over, she removed her lips from her loins and made her way slowly up her torso until she could look directly into her face. She insinuated her legs between Rowena's thighs and pressed her own engorged, lustful pussy lips against hers. Slowly, lovingly, she ground her hips so that the two pairs of love lips performed a tender, pleasure inducing dance with each other. When the girl began to shake and tremble with her impending explosion of lust, she pressed the top of her pussy down as hard as she could against the girl's swollen, distended clit.

Rowena moaned and cried as she came. Her hands gripped her lover as if she feared that she would tumble off of the earth. Antonia's crevasse began to pulse and contract as well and she moaned her pleasure while she watched the contorted face of her lover record her ecstasy. Later, after their doomed love affair ended, as all such doomed love affairs must, Antonia carried with her always the sight of her young lover's face that night knowing that it was something that her masters could never take from her.

The two women made love for the whole two hours of their allotted time. Antonia taught Rowena how to kiss her breasts, telling her, "*Dammi mi sano un bacio, bella,*" and laughing with pleasured joy. Rowena eagerly complied, sucking hard on Antonia's teats until the slave girl moaned and melted before her. Gingerly, Rowena placed her hand on Antonia's gate of pleasure for the first time, reveling in its soft heat, caressing it until Antonia's body shook with pleasure.

When the time came, Greta knocked on the bedroom door lightly. Antonia gave Rowena a soft, gentle kiss and then, with a tear in her eye, turned and presented her braceleted wrists for the blond girl to affix together. Rowena reluctantly complied and then wrapped her arms around her lover, caressing her breasts and kissing the back of her neck. Greta came into the room. "Hurry, hurry," she said quietly. Antonia's gag had fallen to the floor. She picked it up and guided it into the slave girl's mouth. Antonia opened her lips widely to receive it. When it was buckled back behind her head, covering her adoring face down to her chin, she gave her lover one last look of desire and was pulled by the ring on her collar from the room. Rowena fell down on her bed and cried.

For the next six months, every night, or at least most nights, after her father had gone to sleep and after Greta's bath, Antonia spent two hours in Rowena's bed. Some nights they just lay together, enjoying the warmth of each other's bodies, kissing each other lightly, caressing each other's flesh, alone in a world they had made for each other. Other nights, they copulated feverishly, sucking at each other's fevered slits, moaning their pleasures to each other.

Their relationship was a fierce combination of heaven and hell. Rowena longed for her lover all day at school. When she came home, Greta would permit her a kiss or two, but nothing more. The blond girl would suffer every time her lover was escorted into her father's bedroom to suck his prick or to have her cleft plowed by him. Her blood ran cold when she heard her father fucking her through the door to his room at night and Antonia's sometimes fevered cries.

It made her jealous to think that her lover was deriving pleasure from her father's cock. At the same time, she felt sorrow for her lover, forced to kneel over on the bed or spread her legs while her father sawed his cock back and forth inside her, or to kneel on the floor, her arms bound behind her to suckle at his prick.

On the nights that her father took Antonia out with him to parties or to share her with a friend, Rowena stayed in her room crying and pining for her lover. Once, he lent the slave girl to a friend for a whole week. Rowena thought she would go mad. When she finally returned, they made violent love together so loudly, that Greta had to come and tell them to quiet themselves.

Some nights, Rowena's father fell asleep with Antonia in his bed. Greta never disturbed her on those nights lest the master wake and ask her what she was up to. It was only those nights, and they were most nights, that he locked her in her cage after fucking her that she dared to remove the slave girl from his room.

Antonia blessed the time she could spend with her blond lover. She performed her other duties with alacrity and impassioned skill lest she do something to make her master send her away. She sucked his cock until he virtually screamed with joy. She fucked his friends; she proffered her cunt to his prick, squeezing his manhood with her inner muscles so that he groaned.

The only fear that Antonia had, aside from being taken away from her lover, was that Rowena would come to despise her because of her role as a subservient slut. As her father drove his cock back and forth in her crevasse, she worried that the sounds of his passion would make her lover view her with revulsion. And on those occasions that the man drove her to pleasure, for she was, after all, only human and, as a slave girl, trained to a greatly heightened sexual response, she met her lover later downcast, feeling guilty that she allowed herself pleasure from someone other than her.

One day, however, it all came to an end. A poet has said that the world will end not with a bang, but with a whimper, and that is how the end of this torrid love affair came about.

One afternoon, without warning to anyone, while Rowena was at school, a van pulled up outside the house. Two men came to the door and rang the bell. They had a pretty, blond, naked American girl on a leash with them and an authorization, signed by Rowena's father, to take Antonia with them. It seems that the father had grown too used to Antonia and, since there were a thousand Antonia's to pick from to enliven his prurient interests and make his cock hard, he had decided to trade her in for a new model. He had picked the blond out that morning. The dealer said that he would assess Antonia once he had her back at his store and credit him with her trade in value. Rowena's father wasn't worried about being cheated; the dealer's brother sold medical supplies to the hospital system. The new girl would be, for all intents and purposes, free.

Greta cried as she fastened Antonia's wrist bands together. Antonia's heart fell as she was led on a leash from the house. Resistance or protest was unthinkable. Antonia's lips trembled and her knees weakened as they hooded her and placed her in a cage in the back of the van. They did not have time to dawdle or allow any prolonged goodbyes. They had three more deliveries to make before dark.

When Rowena came home and saw that Antonia was gone, she was hysterical. When her father came home, she begged and pleaded with him to bring her back, confessing all that had gone on between them. Her father was horrified and scolded Greta severely. To have his daughter engage in lesbian activities under his own roof was unthinkable. He ordered his daughter confined to her room for two weeks and changed the lock on his slave girl's cage, keeping the key to himself.

Some months later, Rowena and eleven of her friends from the university staged a demonstration outside the headquarters of the National Commission demanding that all slave girls be freed. They were arrested, of course. Almost immediately. The five brave, young men were given long prison sentences. The seven young women, tried within the hour of their arrest no more than fifty yards from where their demonstration had taken place, although a level or two underground, were deprived of citizenship and ordered expelled from the country. That evening, they were loaded, naked, bound and gagged, onto a truck and driven to the border where they were handed over to a Syrian broker with connections in the Middle East.

Rowena and two of her friends were purchased by a wealthy Turk who ran an exclusive, 'special' resort on a small Ionian island off the coast of Asia Minor. Where she went from there is anybody's guess.

Antonia did not have much time to grieve her expulsion from paradise. She was driven to the slave dealer's store and immediately placed in a brutal, week long retraining course. At night, when they were done with her, bound grotesquely in her cell, she cried and cried for her lost love. Her unhappiness was so intense and so visible, that they kept her in the store's dungeons for an extra week so that they could beat it out of her.

Once she had been approved for resale, she was displayed daily in the shop window or in the showroom. Every day that she was not sold she was whipped. It seems that her moroseness was endemic since the dealer finally gave up on her. She was odd lotted out to an itinerant who shopped her around to several whorehouses with no luck. It wasn't that she had lost her beauty. In fact, her dourness lent an aspect of mystery to her mien. However, none of the whorehouses wanted to take a chance on her at least not for the kind of money that the dealer was asking for.

And this is how she ended up kneeling on a platform in a large tent at the Fall Tournament along with fifteen or twenty other second hand sluts. She and the others had been loaded up into cages and transported the seven hours to the fairgrounds. It was the third day that she had been displayed when Drabik came in looking that morning to buy five cheap slaves and the dealer was looking to unload stock. He still had twelve left. She saw him enter. She shook with fear when he examined her, feeling her breasts and thighs, slapping her skin to see how she bruised. He worried her puss until it moistened and shoved his fingers inside her. The dealer let him have her suck at his cock for a few minutes to see what she was capable of. Antonia dared not have the man find her wanting in this respect and, against her own desires, gave him her best efforts.

She sensed that he was a cruel, remorseless man right away. While she had hoped that she would finally find a new master and be relieved of her life as an unsalable commodity, she definitely did not want it to be him. When he agreed to purchase her she started to cry. She was led bound and gagged across the fairgrounds in a coffle with the other girls. When they reached his tent and she was led inside, her heart almost broke.

He wasted no time in binding her hands above her to one of the rafters and pillorying her body with a thick riding crop. He then pushed her to the floor so he could use her. As the man rode her rear entrance, having shoved himself inside with little or no consideration as to her readiness, she knew that if life with Rowena had been heaven, life with this man would be hell.

She knelt now at his feet in the grandstands of the ponygirl tournament. Having led a sheltered existence as a slave girl, she was astounded at what she had seen as the man led her by a leash on her collar through the fairgrounds and now in the grandstands of the clubhouse. She had heard talk of ponygirls from some of the other slaves, but had discounted it, believing them to be tall tales. It was real though. She watched as the naked women, and regardless of what the masters called them, she knew that they were women, dragged their burdens along the track as if their whole beings were devoted to it. It was then that she realized the scope and the power of the system which had stolen all her rights from her and knew that she would spend the rest of her life as a slave girl.

After a while, friends of her new master came by and sat by him in the box. Antonia was ordered to suck their cocks. She didn't know much Russian, but she knew that expression well. She had not been given the chance to freshen up her appearance this morning after two hours of abuse and she knew that she looked like something the cat had dragged in, but she didn't care. They would take her as they found her. As she knelt before the first man and fellated him, her wrists confined behind her, she wondered if she could somehow get her new, dark master to kill her.

Drabik watched the new slave pleasuring one of his soon to be lieutenants. She was good, he had to admit that. But she was a slut like all the others and he soon redirected his attentions to the track. He had a little money on a troika team due up in the next race. He was not a gambler by nature. This was why he was so successful as a killer and why he knew that his plot against Grobgy would work.

His troika team, a beautiful trio of ponies with raven hair and dark skins, much like his new slave girl, won handily. There were no races for the next hour or so that interested him and so he decided to go the Lightning's campsite to see how she was holding up. Antonia had finished giving service to his lieutenants some time ago and was kneeling back at his feet. He affixed her leash to her collar and bid her follow him.

She was a mess and he decided to drop her off at one of the slave stations so that she could get cleaned up. He needed to have his disks affixed to her labia anyway and he could get that done there as well. He also didn't want to have to deal with her long hair every day and so he would have it cut.

There was an appropriate slave relief station located near his tent where all Grobgys's slave girls were serviced but Drabik didn't want to take the time to go back there. In any large gathering like the Fall Tournament, countless slave girls would need to shit, pee and bathe. Some would require attention to their wounds. And since at any large gathering there would also inevitably be a brisk trade in the servile creatures, there had to be facilities for exchanging their disks and, if the owner wanted, even applying a brand, although that was rarely done except by some of the larger whorehouses.

Drabik stopped off at the entrance to the Slave Relief Tents. One tent was for general grooming, showers and the like, another tent took care of markings issues and even had provision for some elementary piercing or tattoos. The third tent was for discipline and other miscellaneous adjustments to a slave's demeanor or physical condition.

A large, heavy set fellow, wide around the waist, wearing a grey peasant's shirt and blue jeans sat at the desk outside the facility.

"I'd like her showered and shampooed," Drabik told the man. "And I want her hair cut to just above her shoulders. Have them leave enough so that if I need to I can get a good grip on her hair." Drabik demonstrated his desire by placing his hand palm down at the side of his slave girl's neck indicating how long he wanted the hair to be when they were done.

"No problem," replied the man as he wrote down Drabik's instructions. "Do you want the hair?" he asked.

"What," Drabik replied.

"The hair," the man repeated, "the hair that's cut off. Do you want it or should I give you a credit for it?"

"You can keep it," Drabik answered. He took two round, flat, golden colored objects from his pocket and put them on the desk.

"Here are my disks. The ones she has right now are dealer's disks. I'd like them replaced."

"Okay," the man said somewhat musically as he wrote down Drabik's desire.

The clerk placed the front page of the form he had been writing on in a clear plastic envelope together with the two small, golden disks, and attached it to Antonia's collar. He gave Drabik the bottom copy and told him, "She'll be ready in an hour, okay?"

The killer nodded and made arrangements for her to be delivered to his tent. After Drabik took his copy of the form, the clerk pulled a plastic strip from a pile on the desk, checked it to see that it matched the number on the work order and then showed it to Drabik. Once Drabik saw that it matched the number on his receipt, the plastic band was clipped to the ring in the front of Antonia's collar and sealed. No one would be able to claim her except the person who held the appropriate corresponding receipt. If you lost it, you had to wait until the end of the event and present proof of ownership. Slave girls held more than a week were sold.

When he arrived at Lightning's campsite Jerzi was sitting by the door of his caravan wearing his racing gear, sans the cap. The slave girl had Lightning bent over on her knees with her legs spread and was gently stroking her rear globes and her hairless crevasse. Lightning was giving off soft moans as she luxuriated in the girl's ministrations.

"So how's the foot," Drabik asked Jerzi. He sat down next to him. Amanda began to rise to get him a refreshment, but he waved her back down. He didn't want anything to drink.

"It's a little sore," the dwarf answered him. "I don't know if you noticed it or not, but she limped a little on her way back to the encampment after her race this morning."

"Yeah, I saw it," Drabik returned. "And I didn't like it. Has Grobgy said anything?"

"What would he say?" Jerzi shot back. "He made his decision a few days ago. Lightning goes on no matter what."

Drabik looked at the flesh of the creature kneeling on the grass not more than fifteen feet away from him. It might as well have been fifteen miles. He watched the small fingers of the slave girl dart in and out of the gap between Lightning's labia and emerge coated in the ponygirl's fluids. "That's where my prick should be," he thought to himself. He yearned to have the pony's soft body pressed against him, to have her moaning at his touch. He knew that he was torturing himself by being here, but he couldn't help it.

Drabik, like any jealous lover, hated the thought of the small statured driver putting his dick inside the object of his passions. He wanted to wring the little man's neck. He couldn't show it, however. Men didn't fall in love with ponies and that was that.

"This next race is going to be a tough one," Jerzi said. "It's the number three seed and she's been getting faster every race. I'm going to have to let Lightning pull out all of the stops. It's that or quit right here."

For a moment, Drabik considered talking to Grobgy about it but he rejected that because, a) Grobgy wouldn't listen and b) he didn't want to see the bastard if he didn't have to. There was something he could do. If the official tournament physician certified her as unable to run, then the tourney would be over as far as she was concerned. He resolved to have someone drop a dime in the doctor's ear.

Lightning's next race was in a little over forty minutes. He decided to go back to the track and watch it. It was better than languishing and suffering in the encampment with her just out of reach. When he got there a pair of landaus were hurtling down the track. He ignored them and ordered a drink from a slave girl. His men had left and as far as he was concerned it was just as well. He wanted to be alone. The slim, small breasted slave girl returned with his tall glass of scotch and soda within a few minutes. Although he probably would be drinking vodka later, he wanted a change of pace. He saw Lightning being driven into the paddock area and he prepared himself to, for the first time, root against her. So far she hadn't lost a race. If she lost this one because of her foot, and that's all that it could be since she had defeated this other pony a few weeks ago, the physician might take her injury more seriously.

Lightning shivered as she stood in the paddock area waiting her turn to enter the track. It was not a shiver of cold, but of lust. The slave girl had brought her to the edge of orgasm five times as she knelt in the encampment. She had been so dazed with unsatisfied passion that although she had heard some voices speaking, she did not know who had visited them. Some of the other drivers were regulars and, although they weren't permitted to use her, they were often invited to make use of her driver's slave girl, whoever it was at the time. She assumed that her driver received the same polite accommodation when he visited the other camps.

The tall, broad shouldered, naked pony stood waiting for the signal to move on. Her pussy burned as if it was on fire. She rubbed her thighs together and shuffled her boots on the ground. The thing of it was, she knew that she would not get relief until the tournament was all over. She recalled it being three days last time and this was the second day. She had one, maybe two more races to run, by her figuring, and then the final, championship one. Her legs felt fine, it was just her damn foot. After each race she had occasion for cursing the scrawny slave girl who had put the stone in her shoe. Afterwards, back at the encampment, when she thought about it some more, she withdrew the curses, hoping that the wretched girl had not suffered too much.

He felt a minor jiggle to her reins and she began to walk forwards slowly. There was a small tug on the left side of her bit and she slanted somewhat to the left, another to her right and she came back to straight ahead. After a few feet, she was turned hard to the left. Lightning could see where she was going even though, because of the small holes in her hood, she couldn't see it well. If it had been solely up to her, she would have made the very same movements as had been dictated by her reins. But it was not up to her. During the race she needed to respond to the most subtle of adjustments to pressure on her mouth and to even the most insignificant slap of the reins. If she was left to her own devices she might screw up the whole race. For instance, when another pony was gaining on her and trying to pass, she would almost certainly speed up to prevent it. But what if the other pony was going to fade after a few hundred meters, or if her driver was decoying her? Then she would destroy her driver's strategy. It was he who knew the other ponies and their drivers; it was he that spent hours trying to determine the best strategy for a race. She merely had to run and obey.

When they pulled up to the starting line, Lightning saw that the other pony was wearing a bright yellow hood. She seemed to remember it. If she was right, she had raced her a little while ago and beaten her. It had been a tough race though. The pony was fast. Lightning dug her right boot deeply into the dirt of the track. As the higher seed, she had the outside rail. She tensed all her muscles and brought her mind to the zone of maximum commitment. The gun sounded, her reins gave a large, decisive snap and she was off.

Jerzi had decided that there was no other way to run the race than to go wire to wire. He wanted a good lead on the other pony and to maintain it all the way through. Lightning did get off to a quick jump. By the ¼ pole she had a half a cart lead. But that was where it held. All through the first lap, the other pony dogged Lightning's heels. Jerzi realized that the driver of the other pony, a young upstart who he did not know very well, was planning at some point to make a dash for the lead, maybe not until the final turn of the race.

The pain in Lightning's foot was near to excruciating. She did her best to ignore it. It was taking its toll, however, and Jerzi took notice of it. She was slowing down almost imperceptibly. The other cart, on their left, was gaining slowly. Jerzi could not believe it. It had settled in his mind so firmly that Lightning would champion again this season that it had been inconceivable that she could lose. He knew that he had to time Lightning's last burst of speed, the expenditure of any and all of her reserves for the right moment.

As the other pony began to nudge ahead, Jerzi waited. With every passing meter, Lightning was falling behind another inch. Jerzi sensed by the feel of the reins that

Lightning did not want to surrender the lead. He was the master though and she was the beast. Her duties did not include thinking. He prayed that she held her discipline for just a little while longer.

There is a saying that youth will have its day. Well, it wasn't today. Jerzi had the other driver pegged just right. He calculated that once the other driver passed Lightning he would figure that the race was won. Everything that Lightning had done was seemingly calculated to get and hold the lead. If she couldn't hold it, she might be finished.

When the yellow hooded pony had pulled ahead by a full length, Jerzi eased up on the reins just a little bit. The rate of gain for the other cart increased. Jerzi waited and waited and waited. And then it happened. The yellow pony's driver let the pony slow. Having more races to run, he was going to cruise to victory in this one. He thought that the race was over.

Increasing a pony's speed is one thing. Maybe the pony had it, maybe she didn't. But it was a simple matter of moving faster. Jerzi, however, had caught the other driver in the midst of a reduction in speed and effort. It was like catching an aircraft carrier with all its planes on the deck or attacking an enemy encampment when they were in the middle of a change of guard.

"Crack!" went Jerzi's whip. He gave the reins a mighty jerk. Lightning had been literally champing at the bit to shift into afterdrive. She surged ahead ignoring all the pain in her foot, everything else but the need to catch and pass the other pony. It took the other driver a few moments to record the fact that Lightning had speeded up. It took another moment or two for him to order his pony to stop slowing down and to speed up. It took the pony a few moments to interpret and understand the contradictory orders, first to slow down and then to speed up. Once the yellow hooded pony had completed her shifting of gears, Lightning had regained the lead. 300, 250, 200, 150 meters to go and Lightning was still in front. The other pony started to gain again. Lightning was so exhilarated with the efforts of pouring her heart out into her feet that she issued a mighty groan, "Arrrrrrrrrgh!" and dug just a little bit harder. When they crossed the finish line, Lightning was still at least one foot ahead.

Now this was a race that the crowd could get their teeth into. A chant started up in the standing room only stands where the most boisterous fans congregated, "Molnya! Molnya! Molnya!" The chant was adopted by the reserve seat patrons and then by the box seats. Grobgy stood in the owner's booth and acknowledged the accolades of his fellow ponygirl devotees. Jake and Irkut were there to watch it too and they were astounded. "You still think that Chocolate can beat her in her own race?" Irkut asked Jake.

Drabik was on his feet. He threw away the betting slip he had purchased for the other pony just to make his wish that Lightning would lose official. In spite of his hope that she would have buckled under the strain, he smiled ear to ear in admiration of her heart and her energy. There was only one Lightning and he was determined not to lose her.

CHAPTER SEVEN

Jake, Tanya and Irkut were sitting in the box belonging to Helena and Vassily Strelnikov. It was about 2 o'clock in the afternoon. Svetlana, the ponygirl doctor, was there as well as Lada and Zoya, Tanya's sisters, and Boris and Ivan, her brothers. They are all one big, happy family. Irkut was telling everyone about Jake's first trip to the milkpony tent. Tanya was laughing uncontrollably, to Jake's annoyance. Svetlana was giving him a knowing look and the girls couldn't stop giggling. Boris and Ivan were intrigued, never having been there themselves.

"So did you go back and see the girl, Katrina," Helena asked Irkut.

"Of course," he answered with a big grin. "That night and last night too. Do you think I would pass that up?"

"Did her milk really taste like cherries," Boris asked, amazed.

"Sure," Irkut replied. "It's faint. You have to eat a lot of cherries to get the flavor in the milk, but it's there. Isn't it Jake," he asked, jutting his elbow into Jake's side. Tanya and the other girls started to laugh again.

Jake smiled in spite of himself. He was not used to being teased, having a reputation as such a rough, tough fixer, but he had been finding that he secretly enjoyed it. It seemed so natural to be sitting here talking to these folks, as if he's known them for years. "Yes, that's right," he answered.

"I think I'll have to get myself producing if I'm going to hold on to you, Jake," Tanya said. "But what flavor would you like?" She laughed again.

"So, did you help with the milkponies?" Lada asked.

"I did," Irkut replied. "Especially with the one, Irina, the one they were having such trouble with. The owner, Gregor, really doesn't have much time to spend with the ponies after they've been milked for the night. At Katrina's insistence, I spent a few hours with Irina. She's must have been a very good runner because she was very passionate. She ran me dry."

The girls giggled again.

"When I went back last night, they told me that she was much easier to handle the next morning. She put up a little fight, but it wasn't as bad as before."

"But what about poor Katrina," Tanya asked him. "Who did she get to fuck?"

It was Irkut's turn to laugh. "I told you I went back last night, didn't I?"

Everyone laughed at that.

It was championship day and everyone was in a festive mood. The Strenilkov box was just a little to the right of the finish line on the track and in the third tier. Their ponies were, of course, out of the running, but it pleased Helena that the team that had defeated her so decisively was in the finals. It was a redemption of sorts.

The broughams had just run and the Grobgy estate had just won itself another championship. As was the custom, the estate owner and the trainers of the ponies all joined it in the racing circle. Jake had watched carefully as Anton Drabik, his nemesis, strutted around it. "I'm going to kill that fucking bastard if I get the chance," Jake thought to himself.

Chocolate had made it too, as had Lightning. Chocolate's last race had been an anticlimax. She had been scheduled to race the winner between the number 3 pony and the number 6. She had already had a difficult race earlier and Dr. Kevsky was worried what another all out effort might do to her leg. The number 3 seed was heavily favored, of course. It had lost to the number 2 the day before and had its back up against the wall, but there was a qualitative difference between those ponies in the first tier, the numbers 1 through 5, and all the ponies thereafter.

The number 3 pony, wearing a sky blue hood, was a good runner, three years from her original home in Slovakia. She had a great form and was known for her ability to pour it on in the last 300 meters of a race. It was exactly the kind of pony that Chocolate didn't need to compete against right now. The number 6 pony was Belgian. She was a little heavy for her class, but could maintain a good, steady pace throughout the race. Her hood was blue, red and yellow.

The race started out as expected. The number 3 pony, her name was Duska, took an early lead The number 6, named Starlight, nipped at her heels but, given Duska's ability to bring it on in the homestretch, was not given much of a chance. Just as Duska went to pour it on, she seemed to trip. Gamely, she took about five more strides and then fell. She had blown a knee. Starlight cruised to victory and a shot in the semifinals. Chocolate had no trouble putting her out of the tournament.

Lightning had had two more races to make it into the finals. She cruised to victory in both, although in her last race, she had limped her way back to her campsite.

On his way to Helena's campsite to keep his promise to Tanya, Jake had stopped by Chocolate's. Irkut was there slapping Jerzi on the shoulder and Ilona, his slave girl, was on her knees giving Chocolate her reward. Shots of vodka were passed all around. Burnham showed up too with the Malaysian slave, Orchid in tow. She didn't look too happy. He was dragging her along on a leash and she had her arms bound behind her and was gagged. Red stripes covered her belly and breasts. Jake assumed that Burnham had been passing her around the owner's booth as an advertisement for his new line of slave girls.

Burnham exchanged razor like glances with Jake.

Jake had all but given up in getting Burnham to agree on a plan for getting Maddy and Jackie out of the country, but he didn't want the billionaire to know that he had. He tried to lay the groundwork for a little deception.

Before Burnham left, Jake took him aside.

"Listen, Mr. Burnham," he said. "I know you're not happy with me right now and I apologize. I want you to know that I've been doing my job."

"Is that so, Jake?" Burnham replied quite hostilely. "You couldn't tell it from where I'm standing."

"I have two or three ideas for getting the girls out once the tournament is over that I want to go over with you."

"Two or three?" Burnham answered. "Is it two or three?"

"Well, there's two plans, really, but one of them has an two options. I don't want to talk about them now for obvious reasons." Jake took a look around to make sure no one was within listening distance.

"We can meet right after the tournament at the estate," Burnham said. "In my office."

"That sounds fine," Jake replied. "I think that we ought to wait a couple weeks before we make the move. Too many people will be watching right after the race. It wouldn't be unusual to send them to winter quarters then and that's where we can pull some kind of switch or something like that."

"Okay, okay, Jake," Burnham agreed. "I'm sorry I was so upset at you the other day."

"It's okay, Mr. Burnham, I know you've got a lot on your mind with your niece and all. I'm sure we can pull this off."

"Yes, well, as you know, Jake, Lightning's very important to me."

Jake wondered if Burnham's use of Maddy's pony name would be classified as a Freudian slip. "I'm sure, Mr. Burnham, as Jackie is to me."

"Right, right," Burnham, answered evasively. "I've gotta get back now to the clubhouse. It's good to see that Chocolate's a winner. Your strategy is paying off."

"Well, it wouldn't have paid off without that 'strumpet' you saw yesterday," Jake pointed out. "She's the one who got the ponygirl doctor, Dr. Kevsky."

"Oh," Burnham said. "Please give your girlfriend my apologies."

"Has Dr. Kevsky given you her bill yet?"

"No, not yet, but if you see her, tell her that she can have anything she wants."

"I'll be sure to tell her. I'm seeing her in a little while." Jake had a bright idea.

When Jake arrived at Helena's campsite, the six ponies were all standing with their collars tied off to the standing poles. Zoya and Lada were whipping them. There was something about seeing the two beautiful young girls tormenting the helpless, orange tailed ponygirls that made Jake cringe. Lada was laying into one with a four foot long switch. The pony danced and moaned loudly as the whip left angry red lines across her thighs, belly and breasts.

"Hello, Jake," Helena cried out.

Tanya rushed over and gave him a big kiss. Vassily and the boys were there as well as Dr. Kevsky. They were sitting around the campfire drinking, what else?

Tanya led Jake to a chair next to her. Svetlana handed him a glass of vodka. Jake lifted it to Helena, "To a grand effort and future success," he said. Everyone lifted their glasses and drank.

"The girls are just finishing up," Helena said. "I told them, only five strokes apiece and to take it easy. They did try hard."

Jake looked over at the orange tailed ponies. Four of them had red stripes across their breasts and bellies and seemed to be doing little dances to help assuage the pain. Zoya and Lada were at work on the other two. As each lash landed, the ponies gave out piteous moans and their bodies flinched. It didn't look to him like the girls were taking it easy.

When the girls finished, they hung their whips on the side of Helena's caravan and came over to the fire. It was dark outside now and the fire cast a friendly glow over everyone. Two of the slave girls were working on a pot, throwing in and stirring up ingredients. Two more were sitting in cages off to the side, looking forlornly out at the group of lucky, free people sitting around the fire. Jake wondered how Lada and Zoya would feel if he hijacked them back to the states to work in a LA whorehouse for a while. But tonight was not a night for debating ethics. He was there as a friend.

Zoya and Lada sat down and were passed shots of vodka. They were eying Jake strangely with what appeared to be devious smiles. Jake ignored it. There was another toast and he threw his vodka back.

Svetlana was sitting to his right.

"Dr. Kevsky, I wanted to talk to you about something."

"Sure Jake," the attractive physician replied. She was wearing her trademark white blouse but had discarded her jodhpurs for a bright red and green, calico skirt that demurely came down to just below her knees. She had very nice legs, Jake thought as he looked at her. "And I've been wanting to talk to you," she replied.

"There's that look again," Jake thought. He sloughed it off.

"You haven't given Mr. Burnham your bill yet," he said. "You performed a miracle."

"Why thank you, Jake," the blond woman answered.

"You should really sock it to him," Jake told her. "He can afford it."

Svetlana looked at him strangely and then at Tanya. She asked her something in Russian. Tanya shook her head and referred the question to her mother and father. They just shrugged their shoulders.

Jake saw their confusion. "I mean you should really stick it to him," he said.

The quizzical looks went around the campfire once more.

"What should I stick on Mr. Burnham?" Svetlana asked.

"No, I don't mean you should stick something on him," Jake said, a little exasperated. "I meant to say that you should shove it up his wazzoo."

There was tittering around the fire. Humored Russian was exchanged with the word 'wazzoo' prominently figured in it.

The doctor was laughing. "What is a wazzoo and what am I supposed to shove up it, Jake?"

Jake was uncomfortable at being the source of so much humor for the group.

"Jake has a great wazzoo," Tanya joked. Everybody but Jake laughed.

"I don't want to talk about Mr. Burnham's wazzoo, Jake, but I'd like to discus yours," Jake heard the doctor say. She had that smile on her face again.

"No, no," Jake said. "I mean give him a big bill!"

"Ohhhhhhh," the physician said. "But what is a wazzoo?'

"It' a figure of speech, like 'that's water over the dam'," Jake replied.

"What dam?" asked Tanya.

"Forget it," Jake said. This was getting more like an Abbott and Costello routine every minute.

"All I meant to say was that if you're going to give that prick a big bill, which he deserves even if only for what he said about Tanya, I have a suggestion on something you can ask for."

Now it was Vassily's turn. "What did he say about Tanya?"

"Nothing, Papa," Tanya said. "That's water over the dam." Everybody laughed.

Jake, hoping to forestall an international incident, ignored Tanya's father.

"What I'm trying to say is that when you send him your bill there's something I want you to ask for."

"And what's that, Jake."

"He's got a new slave girl named Orchid. She's Malaysian. It would be a personal favor to me if you had her instead of him. He's a son of a bitch."

Svetlana smiled. "And how will you pay me, Jake," she asked lasciviously. "I pulled your rocks out of the water."

"My rocks?" Jake replied. "Oh, you mean my nuts. And its not the water, it's the fire."

Everyone looked at Jake strangely. "I'll never get English," Helena said.

"Well, you did," Jake continued. "Pull my nuts out of the fire, I mean. Anything you want."

"Anything?" Svetlana asked, her eyes widened.

Jake looked at Tanya, "Well, er, almost anything."

Again, there was laughter all around.

"Let me tell you a story," Vassily announced. Jake was happy that the spotlight was finally off of him.

The party, such as it was went on for several hours. Jake was feeling quite relieved that Chocolate had made it into the championship race. Now, she had to win one more as did Lightning. It was a load off his shoulders to get this far. It would have been a shame if all that Jackie had sacrificed had gone to waste.

It was about eleven o'clock and the party was winding down when he finally got to speak to Tanya alone. Helena and the girls were bedding down the ponies. Jake appreciated how the firelight gleamed off of their pale white skins and made their ponytails seem like they were aflame. He and his lover had wandered away from the small circle remaining around the fire. Boris and Ivan disappeared with two of the slave girls and Vassily sat there, across from Svetlana, quietly smoking a pipe filled with deep, rich Balkan tobacco. Jake put his arms around Tanya and gave her a kiss.

"Jake," Tanya said, "I'm so happy I met you."

"I'm happy too, Tanya," he returned. He meant it too, even if once he left Kalikastan he would never see her again.

"You're not like Burnham and the others, Jake," she continued. "What are you doing in Kalikastan?"

"It's a long story, Tanya," he answered her. Too long to tell, he thought.

"Are you staying for a long time?"

"I don't know," he said.

"I have this feeling that I won't see you again after tomorrow night."

"I don't know, Tanya. It's really complicated."

"Can I help you, Jake? I get the feeling that you are in some trouble."

Tanya was looking up at him. The light from the campfire, some 30 feet away, was reflected in her eyes. It had been a long time for Jake that someone offered to help him with his troubles. But there was no way he could tell her what the real issues were. The last thing he wanted was to get her caught up in something that could only bring her misery. Even if she fled Kalikastan with him, she would be like a fish out of water. How could she live in the real world without slave girls, ponygirls and the like? It was as much part of her makeup as being in trouble was of his.

"I'm not in any trouble," he told her, sorry to have to lie. "I've just got things I have to do. I can't really talk about them. I don't want you involved."

"I want you to know that I haven't been joking. I love you, Jake and I want to be with you."

"I know, Tanya. For me it's not so simple. But I want you to know that I haven't met anyone that I felt this good around for a very long time. You, your family, it's been a real treat to get to know you. I wish I had met you earlier."

The pretty blond girl wiped away a tear. Jake felt like he was breaking her heart. One more thing to add to his list of regrets about this mission.

"Will I be able to see you tomorrow night?" the girl asked.

"Sure," Jake said. "And tonight too, if you want. We could go to my trailer or yours, if you father doesn't mind."

"No, tonight is for something else, Jake," she said, rubbing her body against him.

"And what's that?"

"You're a very special man, Jake, and the world's not that full of very special men."

"I don't know…" he started to say.

"Please let me finish, Jake, it's important that you understand."

"Okay," he said. A wisp of blond hair had fallen across Tanya's face and he brushed it back.

"I don't think it's any secret that Svetlana has the lusts for you."

"Now, hold on, Tanya, I'm not sure I want to travel where I think you're going."

"Jake, my sisters, Svetlana, my mother, we share a special bond. It's not easy being a woman in Kalikastan. We've had to make some adjustments to certain realities in our society. We didn't invent female slavery or ponygirls, but they're here. The men, well, let's say that they don't have the same kind of commitment to relationships that they do in other cultures. So we have our own relationships and they have special, well, not really rules, but, I'm not sure how to put it."

"Obligations?" Jake suggested.

"Not really obligations, more like a commitment to sharing. Our lives are so close that it's hard for me to conceive of possessing something without sharing it. It's still mine, you see, but it becomes more valuable to me if the women I love have shared in its enjoyment."

"You want me to make love to Dr. Kevsky," Jake more stated than asked.

"I won't be mad if you say no, Jake, but it would make me feel so much more happy that I found you, so when you go, and I can't fool myself into thinking that you will stay here, those closest to me will be able to share my memories of the best things about you."

"The way I fuck?"

Tanya laughed. "Yes, to some extent. It's more like how you reveal who you really are when you fuck. That's what I want to be able to share and relive with someone close to me. Do you understand?"

So many strange things had been revealed to Jake about himself since he had come to Kalikastan, it did not totally surprise him to hear of a new one. The idea of a woman sharing her lover with another and doing it voluntarily, no, more than voluntarily, wanting it, was not something they would understand in Dubuque. But who was to say what a normal culture was? Having sex outside of a relationship was considered bad behavior because of what it did to the relationship, how it hurt the other person and weakened the bond between the two people. But what Tanya was saying was that it would actually strengthen their bond, make her happier to have known him. Shouldn't he leave one good thing behind him in Kalikastan? Maybe he didn't fully understand Tanya's point of view, but he did understand that she meant every word that she said. He wanted to spend the night with Tanya, but they still had tomorrow.

He looked into Tanya's shining eyes. They had tears in them. If it meant so much to her, who was he to deny her? And Dr. Kevsky was no heifer, either. She was a very attractive, very alluring woman. He couldn't understand why he was hesitating. He was never going to see Tanya after tomorrow. Shouldn't he fuck as many women as he could while he could, especially beautiful ones? Wasn't that every man's dream? A biological imperative?

He realized that that was why he was feeling so guilty about it. It was because he wanted to do it too much. Why was that important if it meant so much to Tanya? He placed his hand under her chin and brought her lips to his. "Okay," he said. "For you."

Tanya beamed. "I love you, Jake," she said, and she kissed him again.

The lovers walked back towards the campfire. Dr. Kevsky was sitting there alone, as if by design.

"Is everybody in on this?" Jake asked.

Tanya giggled. "Of course."

When Jake and Tanya reached the campfire, Svetlana gave them a quizzical, humored look. Then her face broke into a warm, compelling smile. Without speaking, she rose from her chair and gave Tanya a kiss and then a huge hug. Tanya emerged with her eyes watering.

The alluring doctor took hold of Jake's hand. "Thank you, Jake," she said. Her hand was warm and soft. Jake was close enough to her to feel the heat of her body. His cock gave a little twitch.

"Come with me, Jake," Svetlana said. There was a tent set up in the campsite off in the corner away from the trailers and the campfire. It was round with a conical top, almost like a circus tent, and with a circumference of about 100 feet. The ponygirl physician pulled Jake towards it.

Jake gave a look back at Tanya. She was just standing here, smiling.

When they got to the tent, Svetlana opened the flap over the door and brought Jake inside. The interior was lit by several small lanterns hung around the sides. Large, comfortable pillows were strewn about. The floor was covered by a soft, plush, maroon rug. A small table sat in the middle with the center post running through it. There was an elegant, ceramic carafe and two small, crystal tumblers atop it. A bowl of fruit had been placed next to the carafe, containing soft, ripe peaches, dark, almost purple cherries and large, plump oranges. Large, wide, two foot high, wicker baskets were distributed around the circumference of the tent containing a beauteous assortment of red, blue, yellow and purple wildflowers

"All this for me?" Jake asked, trying to break the ice. He had to admit, he was a little nervous.

"Helena had the tent set up this afternoon by the boys. Lada and Zoya got the fruit and Tanya made arrangements for the flowers. The carafe is from me."

"I guess that everyone knew I would say yes but me," Jake said.

Svetlana laughed. The dim light shimmering from the lanterns gave the woman a mysterious, exotic mien. She was still holding Jake's hand. "Let's sit down and have something to drink. It'll help relax you. It's a special recipe."

Jake sat down near the small table, crossing his legs, Indian style. Svetlana drew her long, shapely legs underneath her and knelt next to him. The carafe had a stopper on the top. She took it out and poured some of the liquid in both glasses. It was thick and golden hued, almost like honey, but more translucent. Jake picked up his glass and held it to his nose. It had a piquant, spicy aroma, redolent of cinnamon and cloves. He took a little sip.

"Whoa," he said. "That packs a wallop."

"It's an old family recipe that's been, let's say, beefed up by me," the handsome woman replied. She held up her glass. "To love," she toasted.

Jake held his up and clinked his glass lightly against hers. "To love," he repeated.

"Take it down all at once Jake, like this," Svetlana instructed. She tilted her head back and poured the two ounces or so of liquor back into her throat.

Jake, not to be outdone, followed suit. The substance burned on the way down, but its aftertaste was pleasant. He felt a mild swoon from its effects, almost like he had slugged down a glass of codeine. His chest, though, felt warm and his body felt tingly.

"What's in that stuff," he asked.

"It's a trade secret," the Svetlana replied. "But it'll help fortify you for the task ahead. Have another one."

She had already taken his glass out of his hand and poured another two ounces.

"What about you?" Jake asked.

"You're the one who's going to need to be fortified, Jake."

Looking in the woman's eager eyes, Jake had no doubt of the truth of her statement. Well, he wasn't about to turn down something that might make his evening more enjoyable. He tossed it back.

Svetlana took the glass from him and put her hand on his thigh. "I want you to know, Jake, that this means a lot to all of us. Even Tanya's father. He knows how important it is to Tanya's happiness."

"I'm not sure I understand it," Jake answered. "But I wouldn't be doing this if I didn't believe it was true."

A devilish smile broke out onto Svetlana's face. It was accentuated by the flickering, faint light. "You mean that you wouldn't have succumbed to my charms any other way?"

"Oh, I'm not saying that," Jake answered somewhat tentatively. He had the feeling that he was venturing into be careful what you say territory. And the effects of the second glass of the golden hued concoction were making him a little light headed. He was not really certain that drinking a second glass had been a good idea.

Svetlana removed her hand from Jake's thigh and began to unbutton her stylish but conservative, white blouse.

"Are you saying that if I showed you my breasts that you wouldn't be tempted to caress them?" She had all the buttons undone very quickly and she pulled the blouse open, revealing a pair of pale, firm breasts, much more than a handful each. She was wearing a lacy, silk bra that barely covered her areolas. The very desirable globes shimmered in their captivity while she pulled her blouse free from the waistband of her skirt and then lowered it down her arms. She cast it to the side and then reached behind her to unfasten her bra.

Jake was looking on, mesmerized. Watching a woman undress was astoundingly sexy, especially such an elegant, desirable woman like the doctor. It was nice seeing all the available, naked flesh of the almost uniformly beautiful and shapely slave girls running around, but watching a woman take off her clothes was something that he was discovering that he missed. Watching Tanya disrobe had been enthralling. Watching the more mature and self confident blond woman do the same was even more so.

The tall, shapely woman drew her bra away from her breasts and let the soft, smooth, glistening, silk straps slide down her arms. She tossed the garment aside. Her breasts, now free, seemed to glow in the dim light. Her nipples were hard with desire, sitting atop broad, smooth, reddish circles.

She leaned over towards Jake, letting her loose, heavy globes sway beneath her.

"And if I had put my lips to yours like this," she said, pressing her wide, soft lips onto his, her tongue darting out and teasing his mouth provocatively, and then pulling slowly away, "would you have said no to me then, Jake?" She didn't give him time to answer. She brought her lips to bear again and circled her hand behind Jake's head. Her lips were parted and Jake's separated as if by their own will. Her hot tongue slid enticingly into his mouth and conjoined his. Jake placed his hands on her hips and then ran them over her soft, bare back. Svetlana moaned her growing passion into his mouth.

After a long exchange of lust, the half naked, blond woman eased herself back and then stood. She had slipped her shoes off of her feet. Her skirt fastened at the side and she moved her delicate, long hands to undue it. Jake sat as if lost in a haze, watching her, finding her more and more attractive by the moment.

"If, I had removed my skirt like this Jake," she said, stepping out of it, "and my panties," she added, drawing the delicate, white garment down her long thighs, over her knees and down to her feet, stepping out of them gracefully, "would you have said no to me then?"

The somewhat befuddled American 'fixer' stared at the naked form of the mature woman. Her curves were softer than the mostly younger women he had bedded since he came to Kalikastan, excluding the bird-woman, Betty, of course. Her breasts did not stand up quite so energetically on her chest, but draped slightly, giving an aura of luxuriousness. Her blond bush was untrimmed, but it was light and sparse and he could clearly make out the forms of her love lips. Her thighs were firm but soft and her hips were wider than the younger girls, but not overly so, just enough, in fact to give emphasis to her taut belly and to suggest the pleasure awaiting anyone who matched their hips to hers.

Svetlana stared at Jake unabashedly. There was nothing demure about her. Her sexuality was frank and undisguised. She had her hands on her hips and stood there, her feet ajar, one slightly ahead of the other. She was clearly conscious of her beauty in an unabashed way. Her mannerisms and posture bespoke a sexual experience that would well benefit anyone who had the fortune to supp at her fonts.

"Well, Jake," she said, "Would you have said no if you had seen me like this?"

Jake hesitated for just a moment and said, "No."

Svetlana smiled. Her hair was just below shoulder length and she shook it now unconsciously, her only girlish mannerism so far. When she moved her head, her breasts swayed sending a wave of lust through him.

The tall, lovely woman gracefully knelt before Jake and took hold of one of his boots. "It's time to get you naked, too, Jake," she said. He sat there virtually paralyzed as she slid both of his boots off of his feet together with his socks. Svetlana moved her body between Jake's now outstretched legs. Her knees between his thighs, she pressed her lips to his, sliding her hot tongue across them, while she took hold of his shirt and began to unbutton it. When she was finished, she placed her hands on his near hairless chest and caressed it. Jake put his arms around her and pulled her naked body to him. Her breasts crushed against his bare chest as their mouths worked hungrily against each other's.

Something seemed to snap between them at that moment. Svetlana dropped her hands to Jake's belt and hurriedly began to unbuckle it. Jake sloughed off his shirt, pulling it down off of his wrists. He lifted himself so that he could draw his pants down. The beautiful physician pulled them off of him lustfully. Their bodies and mouths met and they were off.

There was little time spent on preliminaries for either of them. They fell to their sides and it was nip and tuck as to who would take the top position, but Jake, because of his greater strength and, perhaps, wilder passion, won out. Svetlana spread her vulva open with her hand so that he could pierce it. She was well into her excitement and his cock passed easily inside.

Both of them grunting and groaning, their bodies slapping against each other's, the couple let their lusts bear them away. Jake gave his hips mighty thrusts, working his thick prick along the doctor's hot, velvety passage. Their lips were joined fiercely together as if, had they parted, they would have flown off into space. Svetlana raised her legs and circled them behind Jake's back. Her womanly arms held his body fiercely down onto hers. Their tongues writhed together, relishing every point of contact.

Svetlana came first. She uttered a gasp and her hips began thrusting madly back at Jake's. "Uuuuuuummmmm! Uuuuuuummm! Uuuuuuummmmm!" she moaned as her pussy throbbed and pulsed around Jake's meat. It was too much for him to take, and his cock began to send jolting stabs of ecstasy through him. "Arrrrrrrrgh! Aaaaaaauuuuuugh! Aaaaaauuuuuughhh!" he groaned, becoming more overwhelmed by passion by each powerful spurt of his fluids into the welcoming crevasse.

When their fires had cooled, the two lovers lay enwrapped in each other's arms for a long time. Their hearts beat together like sympathetic drums, their chests heaved against each other. Gradually they began to recover lucidity. Jake's head lay next to hers, resting on her shoulder and Svetlana caressed it softly, virtually purring in her satisfaction. "Oh, Jake," she said, "everything that Tanya said was true. You are one great fuck!"

"I can say the same thing for you, Svetlana. You really set me on fire."

The beautiful, blond doctor rolled Jake's body off of her gently. "Let's have another drink, Jake," she said, "and then I'm going to suck your cock."

Jake laughed. The couple reformed near the small table in the middle of the tent. Svetlana poured them both a glass of the honey colored liquor.

Svetlana raised her glass. "To lust," she said.

"To lust," Jake repeated, and they clinked their glasses together. When Jake had downed his, she poured him another glass.

"No, that's all right," Jake said. "This stuff makes me a little woozy."

"Doctor's orders, Jake," Svetlana insisted.

"You're trying to get me drunk, Svetlana. Do you plan to take advantage of me?" Jake said jokingly.

"Something like that, Jake, now bottoms, up."

Jake, exhilarated by his tryst with the delectable woman, shot his glass back once more. He felt a wave of euphoria pass through him.

"Boy, what's in this stuff," he asked.

"Magic," Svetlana returned. She put her hands on his shoulders and pushed him to the soft floor of the tent. Extending her long, voluptuous body next to him, she pressed her breasts against his side and stroked her hand across his firm, muscled chest, over his taut belly and down to his loins. Her hand took possession of his tool and its heat sent a shiver of delight through him. His cock regained its strength quickly. Jake was pleasantly surprised at his rapid comeback, but you don't look gift horses like that in the mouth, especially when a beautiful mouth was kissing your chest, your stomach and then spread itself around your needy pole.

"Ooooooooh," Jake moaned as Svetlana ran her tongue around the shaft of his cock. Her right hand was cupping his scrotal sac and her left was caressing his chest and stomach. Jake remembered the doctor's threat of yesterday that she would make him suffer tantalizingly on the brink of orgasm for a long time before granting him release. He anticipated the delicious suffering it would entail.

Svetlana shifted position, maintaining her mouth's possession of Jake's cock, sliding herself over his thigh until she knelt between them. As her mouth worked slowly up and down his crank, she caressed his tight, strong thighs, spreading his legs widely. On each upward stroke, she swirled her tongue around the meaty head of the rigid pole and then descended slowly once again.

Jake did not know how long the doctor made him teeter on the edge of ecstasy. It's hard to keep track of time when a beautiful, desirable woman has your cock in her mouth. Svetlana seemed to have superior knowledge of male anatomy. When his cock seemed ready to jet into space, she withdrew her lips and kissed his thighs, his belly, his chest, while her hands found the little niches in his muscles and kneaded them until he groaned from the quite pleasurable pain. When he had been distracted sufficiently from his desire to climax, she returned to her primary task, the delivery of pleasure to his manhood with her lips, mouth and tongue.

When he came, Jake's moans resounded through the large tent. His heels dug little trails in the soft rug. His hands gripped his tormentor's tightly as she extended them to assuage his glorious agony. Jake felt like his insides were pouring out of him through his cock. He could not remember ever coming like that before and he had had some quite accomplished lips and mouths on his tool over the last eight months. The doctor's treatment had been wondrously successful.

The sated man lay in a near comatose state for a long time. Svetlana lay beside him, feeding him an occasional, plump, juicy cherry from which she had removed the pit with her teeth or a delicious, juicy section of orange. It was funny. He felt sated, his body was way beyond relaxed, but he felt energized, as if he could go another round with Svetlana without any trouble at all.

Svetlana excused herself a moment, to get another pillow, she said and he sensed one of the lanterns being moved towards the door. He thought nothing of it, lost, as he was, in a post orgasmic haze. The shapely, soft skinned, voluptuous woman returned to her spot beside him and slid a pillow under his head. She then draped herself across his chest and began to give him delicate little nibbles at his lips. Jake ran his hand down her silken hair lazily. Just then, he felt a pair of delicate, female hands sliding up his shins and over his thighs. He was too dazed to respond, but when a pair of soft lips encircled his manhood, he groaned.

"Who…" he said weakly.

"Shhhhhhhh!" Svetlana interrupted. "It's magic, remember? I can kiss your lips and suck your cock at the same time," she whispered.

The mouth on his cock was suckling him lazily. The surprising thing was that his cock was readily responding. "Ahhhhhhh," he sighed. He did not for even a moment believe Svetlana's explanation, but the pleasure he was receiving was too great to gainsay her. Something was going on, he knew it. There was something in the golden liqueur that was stoking his lusts and heightening his experience of pleasure.

After a while, after causing him to groan and his legs to tremble from pleasure, the mouth on his cock abandoned its task. He felt sultry lips ascending his belly preceded by soft, hot hands. Svetlana gave him a kiss and moved to the side. Large, fluffy breasts with stiffened nipples caressed his chest and tender lips found his own. His hands caressed the woman's soft hips and back as she spread herself over him, maximizing the contact with his energized flesh. They kissed for a long time. Jake's mind was trying unsuccessfully to identify his lascivious assailant. The body was young, the hair was blond. He decided it was Tanya, come to reclaim her lover. He kissed her fervently, clasping her body closely to his. He had never felt such strong desire for a woman before. She slid her legs up until her knees were even with his hips. Her pussy, wet with arousal, dragged along his yet again, stiff cock. He felt her hips rise and a woman's hand guide his manhood to her soft, yearning cleft. He knew it was Svetlana, lending a helping hand to the lovers, since he also felt two feminine hands on either side of his head, caressing him softly while his tongue danced in the woman's mouth.

When she started her motions above him, her pussy clenching hard on his cock with every downward stroke, their lips separated. She groaned with pleasure. Jake became confused. It sounded like Tanya's sigh of pleasure, but it was somehow deeper, more resonant. And the breasts which pressed against his chest were larger and softer than Tanya's. Jake placed his hands on the side of the head of the woman riding his cock and raised it so that he could see her face. The light was dim, but it was clearly not Tanya. It was Zoya, her elder sister. She was giving his cock long, languorous strokes with her cunt. Her face was a mask of passion. She smiled at him, a mischievous, sultry smile. "Ohhhhh, Jake," she moaned, "I love your cock. Ohhhhhhh, fuck me, Jake! Make me come! Ohhhhhhhhh!"

Jake's hips were responding assiduously to the motions of Zoya's hips Svetlana was lying next to them, on Jake's right, stroking his head and kissing his neck. It was too late for Jake to stop or protest, his lusts were too far gone. Zoya was using her cleft expertly to pleasure his stiff rod while grinding her hardened love button against his pelvic bone each time her pussy swallowed him to the hilt.

His mind was luxuriating in the pleasure that Tanya's sister was bringing him when another warm, female body appeared on his left. A mouth began to kiss his neck on that side and then rose up over his chin and claimed his lips. She was nestled in Jake's left shoulder and he was able to run his hand down her smooth, soft, shapely torso. Her breasts were pressed against his side. From the size of the breasts and the slenderness of the hips, Jake knew that it was the eighteen year old Lada.

It seemed like he had hit the trifecta, scored a hat trick, hit a triple. Three, delicious, blond women were pleasuring his body, three free, uninhibited women, unashamed at their lust. Zoya's moan brought him back to business. His cock was ready to explode once more. Now he knew that Svetlana's potion was stoking his flames. He was virile, but not Superman. Zoya screeched loudly, announcing her cresting passion. Her pussy clenched and released his cock in powerful waves. Her hips were working atop him frantically. "Oh, Jake! Oh, Jake! Keep going! Keep going! Don't come yet! Not yet! Ahhhhhhhhh!" she cried. She was gyrating her hips madly, enjoying the feel of his steel hard prick in her crevasse. She pumped her hips up and down over him about ten more times and yelled, "Oh, god! Now! Now, Jake! Fill me up! Give me your cum!"

Jake groaned and complied, as any gentleman would. The two of them filled the tent with their lustful cries.

Zoya collapsed on him as her orgasm receded. Lada and Svetlana continued to nuzzle and kiss him. His body felt warm and light, like he was floating on a cloud of pleasure.

"You devils," he finally was able to moan. "You planned all this,"

"Mmmmmmmmmmm, yessssss," Lada moaned in his ear. And I'm next."

"I don't think that…."

"Don't think, Jake," he heard Svetlana say, "enjoy!"

Lada gave him a sweet but impassioned kiss. "Tanya says that you really know how to give delight with your mouth, Jake," she said softly, almost wistfully. "I want you to show me. I want you to lick my pussy until I come. Please, Jake, Please!"

"Tanya…" Jake started to say.

"She'll be here soon, Jake," Svetlana said. "It's Lada's turn now. Make her come with your mouth."

Jake's cock stirred at the lascivious command. Zoya slid off him to enable him to turn and give Lada his attentions. She kissed him, her hands on the side of his head, and then pulled him towards her as she shifted to her back. He slid his chest over her and his legs between her thighs. Her hands flitted lightly over his shoulders and back. Slowly, he brought his lips down her neck and then over her chest. He took her nipples in his mouth, one after the other and suckled them until she moaned. Her breasts were firm and pert, with conical tips. He relished the taste and feel of her hardened teats in his mouth, the warmth of her belly against his chest, the firmness of her thighs as they pressed against his hips. As he ran his lips down her belly towards her labial divide, his hands caressed the sides of her torso and slid over her narrow, graceful hips. He lavished his kisses over her lower belly, stroking her skin with his tongue. Her hands were on his head, gently urging him to his ultimate goal. "Mmmmmmmmm," she moaned softly. Her hips shifted slightly and her body quivered. He brought himself lower and lower until his lips brushed across the small patch of pubic hair over her sex and then took possession of her already stiff clit.

"Ohhhhhhhhh!" she moaned as he tickled it with his tongue. Her hand clasped his hair tightly and her thighs split wide. "Ohhhhh, Jake," she said lustfully.

The impassioned fixer spent a long time pleasuring Lada's loins. He dragged his tongue the length of her slice and massaged her tender inner thighs with his hands. He drove his tongue deep into her cleft while stroking her love button softly with his thumb. He brought her to the edge of climax twice, pulling back just as her hips rose and her thighs pressed against his head. She moaned with frustration, but when he resumed, her sighs and groans of pleasure had redoubled. Finally, he let her come. "Oh! Oh! Oh!" she yelled as her pussy pleasured her. "Oh, Jake! Don't stop! Don't stop!"

After her third quaking orgasm, Lada finally sighed, satiated. Jake rose slowly from his position between her thighs, kissing her belly and her breasts and then her still panting lips. She looked at him dreamily and stroked his head, not saying a word.

To Jake's amazement, his cock was hard again. He looked up. Zoya and Svetlana, having had ringside seats for Jake's demonstration of his cunnalinguist skills, were leaning against each other. Zoya had her hand on Svetlana's pale, white thigh and the older woman was stroking Zoya's fluffy, left breast. Then Jake realized here was someone else in the room. He turned and saw Tanya kneeling near the table in the center. She had doffed her clothes and was smiling at him lovingly, her eyes wet with tears. Jake rose and embraced her.

"Oh, Jake," she said. "That was so beautiful. Thank you."

Their lips melded together, their bodies joined. Jake reveled in her taste, her smell, her warmth. When they broke, Svetlana was holding out to them two glasses of her magic elixir. Jake took one in hand as did Tanya and they both downed them simultaneously. Jake's throat burned as the substance went down but his body exulted. He placed his glass on the table and advanced to his lover, pushing her by the shoulders to the soft, dark rug. He stroked her face while staring down at her. "Tanya..." he started to say.

She put her fingers on his lips, silencing him. "Wait until tomorrow, Jake," she said. "Tell me tomorrow. Just make love to me now."

Reinvigorated by the potion, Jake made love to Tanya for a long time. He kissed her body, stroking it, loving it, until she moaned with excitement. When he entered her, she groaned. He had the back of her knees locked into the crux of his arms and lifted them until her knees touched her breasts. She had her arms around his neck. He fucked her with long, powerful strokes.

Later, he remembered shifting positions with her several times. He recalled her moaning her pleasure to him more than once. He remembered coming in her while she was bent over on her knees, her thighs spread, her head and arms lying on the rug.

After that, it was more or less a blur. Svetlana fed him another glass of her concoction and he remembered, at one point, having his face between her thighs, returning her favor. One of the blond women, he thought it was Zoya, perched herself above him, head to tail and sucked his cock while he pleasured her with his lips and tongue. Lada spread her thighs for him and he plowed her dainty, tight crevasse while she moaned her delight, shifting, at her imperative instructions, to her small, rear hole. He was afraid of splitting the small, young girl's back passage, but Svetlana, lovingly applying a lubricant to his cock, assured him, laughing, that Lada would be quite accommodating to him there. She was right, and the tight orifice welcomed him easily. Lada, on her hands and knees, bucked wildly against him while she came, sending him into another paroxysm of delight.

After that, someone washed off his cock with warm, soapy water and he made love to Tanya again. Later, he rested for a while, watching Svetlana and Lada make love to each other. The diminutive girl appeared child like in the arms of the mature, older woman. But she screamed with pleasure when Svetlana kissed her between the thighs. He wasn't sure, and was afraid to ask, but he thought he remembered lying back against Svetlana's gentle, voluptuous breasts, her hand gently working his tool, watching Tanya and Zoya kissing each other fervently, their hands buried in each other's pussies, moaning until both of their bodies began to shake and quiver with pleasure.

When he awoke in the morning, Tanya was lying next to him, her arm draped across his chest, their legs intertwined. Svetlana, Zoya and Lada were spooned against each other, in that order, their descending size making them seem like x-rated babushka dolls.

His motions awoke his lover and they kissed each other tenderly.

"How do you feel?" Tanya asked.

It was odd, but Jake did not feel hung over at all. "I feel fine," he said. "How about you?"

"Oh, I feel wonderful, Jake. I'm so happy. You're not mad at me are you?"

"Not in the least," Jake answered her, giving her another kiss. "That was the most amazing night I've ever had. Your sisters and Svetlana were delightful."

"I know that they enjoyed you too. I'm glad you gave us this night to share with each other. We'll be comparing notes for a long time."

Jake laughed.

Svetlana stirred and then Lada. The older woman smiled at Jake. She too asked him how he was feeling.

"I feel fine," Jake answered. "What was in that stuff?"

"Oh, a little of this and a little of that. It's something from an old folk remedy that I've improved upon in my lab. I only bring it out on special occasions. I've given a modified recipe to Tanya's brothers and her father so that they can service the ponygirls."

"Well, it sure worked for me," Jake said, smiling. "If you bottled it, it'd be worth a fortune."

"Oh, I prefer to keep it our little secret. You'll respect that, won't you Jake?"

"Of course," he said.

Lada, having now come fully awake, dashed across the tent and placed her arms around Jake, pressing her warm, naked body against him. "I'm so happy that Tanya met you, Jake. I had a great time."

"So did I, Lada," Jake replied, returning her embrace.

"There's only one problem," she said, giving a small frown.

"What's that," Jake answered.

"I didn't get to suck your cock." She pushed him over playfully and covered his body with hers.

He started to push her off. "I don't think..." he started to say. It seemed that if he continued his relationship with these lusty women he would hardly ever be able to complete a sentence.

"Well, Jake," Tanya interrupted, "it's only fair." Laughing, she pressed her body on top of Jake's holding him down. Svetlana, giving a quite unmatronly giggle, joined her. Lada lowered herself on Jake's body and deftly subsumed his soft prick into her mouth. She began to work it expertly.

While Lada sucked his cock, Tanya and Svetlana took turns dipping their hot tongues in is mouth while caressing his chest and belly. Zoya, awoken by the commotion, came over to see what she was missing. Producing one of her mischievous smiles, she joined in, running her lips and tongue across his belly and then giving him one of her fluffy, pale breasts to suckle on.

Consistent with his heroic performance the night before, Jake rose to the occasion again. Soon Lada and the other women had him moaning and writhing beneath them. Lada's small mouth made a tight fit on his cock and her lips pressed against his solid shaft hard. She had his balls in her hand, caressing them, urging them to grant her a taste of his elixir. He came with a groan and spurted his essence into her mouth while Tanya, Svetlana and Zoya continued to pleasure him. They ceased only when Lada raised her young, blond head and announced gaily, "Mmmmmm-mmmmm! I'm done." While Jake enjoyed the fading echoes of his pleasure, the three other women laughed.

To be continued...